UNTANGLE MY HEART

IONA ROSE

Untangle
My Heart

Publisher: Some Books
ISBN- 978-1-913990-22-0

AUTHOR'S NOTE

Hey there!

Thank you for choosing my book. I sure hope that you love it. I'd hate to part ways once you're done though. So how about we stay in touch?

My newsletter is a great way to discover more about me and my books. Where you'll find frequent exclusive giveaways, sneak previews of new releases and be first to see new cover reveals.

And as a HUGE thank you for joining, you'll receive a FREE book on me!

With love,

Iona

Get Your FREE Book Here:
https://dl.bookfunnel.com/v9yit8b3f7

Chapter One

SEBASTIAN

I take a subtle look at the woman standing next to me at my front door. She's saying something, something I don't hear, and then she giggles, not seeming to notice or care that I don't respond.

She's drunk, but not so drunk that I'm taking advantage of her by bringing her back to my place. It was her who kept ordering more cocktails after the work dinner. It was her who slipped her shoes off beneath the table and ran her toes up my leg inside of my trousers. She might be a little bit tipsy, but she knows exactly what she wants. Me.

She's tall. Almost as tall as me, and she holds herself with confidence. A lot of tall women slouch, wanting to not stand out, but not Natalie. No, Natalie wants to be seen, to be noticed. Well she's going to love tonight because fuck me I see her. I see her willowy waist, her full breasts and her long legs. I see the lust in her eyes and the glisten of moisture on her lips where she keeps licking them seductively.

Oh I see her alright, and pretty soon, I'll be seeing a whole lot more of her. Natalie catches me watching her as I miss the lock with the key. She smiles, a smile that sends a blast of fire through me. It's the smile of a predator about to devour their prey. I'm good with that. I am most definitely open to being devoured by that sensual mouth of hers.

"Is something distracting you Sebastian?" she asks, faking innocence even as she tugs at her top, revealing a little more cleavage.

I let out a soft laugh.

"Whatever gave you that impression?"

"I thought maybe you were thinking about our potential merger," Natalie smiles putting all of the emphasis on the merger.

I finally manage to unlock the door. It's not the smooth move I would have liked, but it sure doesn't seem to have put Natalie off. I can almost smell the lust coming off her in waves.

"Oh I think our merger is a sure thing," I reply as I step inside my house and stand aside so Natalie can enter.

She laughs and twiddles a strand of her silvery blonde hair around one finger. She looks down for a second and then looks up at me through her lashes, her smile widening.

"How about the tour first?" she asks.

"Sure," I grin.

I would have preferred to have gotten straight down to business so to speak. It's not like Natalie was going to be anything other than a one night stand. Why does she want to see every room of my house? The only room she needs to see is my bedroom. Still, it won't take too long. Why not?

"So what's down there?" she asks, pointing to a door off the hallway with a set of wooden steps leading down to a basement.

"Oh that's where I keep the bodies of those who have double crossed me," I laugh.

"No seriously? What's down there?" she pouts. "I bet it's a flashy wine cellar isn't it?"

"Not exactly," I laugh. "I'm more of a bourbon man."

When it's clear to me she isn't going to relent and just let me whisk her off to the bedroom, I bite back the sigh and lead her to the stairs. I lead her down, pulling on the light as I step inside the door. Natalie laughs when we reach the bottom of the stairs and she sees the room.

The basement covers the entire length and width of my house in one room, and I've made it into a games room. There's a full size pool table, several pinball machines, a dart board and a few video game machines. There's also a well stocked bar in the corner, several high stools lining it, and half a dozen bean bags scattered around the room. I decide to make the most of the tour. I head for the bar and pour out two large bourbons. I hand one to Natalie who sips it and makes a face and then laughs.

"It's strong," she says.

"What can I say? I thought I'd get you drunk and take advantage of you," I grin.

"Works for me," she laughs.

I begin to relax a little as I sip the bourbon. Natalie is a sure thing. She hasn't asked for the tour because she's having second thoughts. She's just nosey. I can deal with nosey.

"So, do you want to continue the tour or do you want me to kick your ass at pool first?" I ask.

She glances over at the pool table and then she smiles and shakes her head.

"The rest of the tour sounds good. I can do without the humiliation of being thrashed at pool," she says.

I lead the way back upstairs.

"Yeah people say I'm pretty good with my balls," I say, looking back over my shoulder and winking at Natalie.

"Oh I bet you are," she grins back.

I reach the top of the stairs and take her into the lounge. It's a reasonable sized room, with brown leather sofas, an entertainment system, a coffee table, and little else.

"Wow you like the whole minimalist thing don't you?" Natalie remarks.

"What more would I need in here?" I ask, genuinely curious as to what she thinks is missing.

"I don't know. The little things that make a house a home," she says. She smiles. "This is such a bachelor pad. You need a woman's touch."

"The only place I need a woman's touch is ..." I trail off, nodding towards my crotch.

Natalie laughs and shakes her head, but she moves closer to me. I can smell the bourbon fumes on her breath when she whispers into my ear.

"That can definitely be arranged."

"You know what?" I say. "Let's finish the tour right here. The kitchen is a kitchen. Normal. Boring. My office is a no go area. So we may as well just head upstairs right now."

I don't wait for her to respond. I turn and walk from the lounge, heading for the stairs. I know she's following me, eager to get to the good bit herself now. I reach the top of the stairs and lead her along another hallway.

"Bathroom. Linen closet," I say pointing out doors as we pass them. "Spare bedroom. Another spare bedroom."

"You know if you get bored of the corporate world, you would make an excellent tour guide," she laughs.

"I aim to please," I reply.

I reach the end of the hallway and stop outside of the final door. I throw it open with a flourish.

"And the only room you really wanted to see. My bedroom."

Natalie gives me another one of those lust filled grins that makes my cock twitch, and steps into the bedroom. She looks around for a moment and then nods her approval. Obviously the addition of a wardrobe and a chest of drawers makes this room more suitably furnished to Natalie's tastes. She misses the point in my opinion. It's all still practical stuff. There is nothing in this room that distinguishes it from a soulless hotel room.

"Are you going to stand in the doorway all night then or are you coming in?" Natalie asks.

She downs the last of her bourbon and puts the glass down on the chest of drawers. I step into the room and kick the door closed behind me. The moonlight streaming in the window gives us enough light to see by and I don't bother switching the light on. I down the rest of my own bourbon and stand my glass beside Natalie's.

I go to her and pull her into my arms. My lips find hers and it's like my kiss breathes life into her. She wraps her arms around me, her hands running up and down my back. Her mouth is hungry for me, her tongue probing into my mouth as her hands make their way beneath my shirt.

I run my hands down Natalie's body, feeling the curve of her hips. I move one hand between us and rub my fingers over her mound. She's wearing loose fitting trousers, but she still moans at my touch. She presses herself tighter against my hand, moving her hips slightly.

She pulls her mouth from mine and kisses down my face, over my jaw and down my neck. Her kisses bring goose bumps to the surface of my skin. She steps back from me and begins to unbutton my shirt. She pulls it down my arms and lets it drop to the floor and then she looks me up and down. She nods approvingly when she sees my abs and I bite my lip to stop myself from smirking.

She runs her nails lightly over my chest and I increase the pressure on her mound. I lean in and kiss her again, walking her backwards towards my bed. When her legs hit the mattress, she breaks our kiss long enough to kick her heels off, hop up onto the bed and scoot backwards. I join her eagerly, wanting to get her out of those clothes, to taste her pussy.

Our lips lock again as I reach down and begin to open her trousers. I have barely gotten the button open when my cell phone rings loudly in my pocket, making us both jump.

"Ignore it," Natalie breathes.

Like I was going to do anything else. She finishes opening her trousers and pushes them down, kicking them away. Her legs have a light tan, and they're every bit as long as I imagined them to be. I trail my fingers up one of her inner thighs. I run my fingers over her panties, feeling the clinging dampness of them. Oh she wants me alright. I push her panties to one side and slip my fingers inside of her lips. My cock hardens as I feel how wet she is. How ready for me.

Natalie gasps as my fingers find her clit. I begin to work her, listening to her gasps as I bring her close to the edge. My cell phone rings again.

"Goddammit," I shout, pulling my hand away from Natalie and slamming my fist down on the mattress between us in frustration.

I pull my phone out of my pocket, ready to cut the call off and turn the damned thing off. It's Matt, my older brother. It has to be important for him to be calling at this hour. He's not going to quit calling until I answer, and if I ignore him, he'll start on the landline.

"Fuck," I say quietly.

Natalie grabs my hand and tries to move it back down to her pussy. I pull it away gently.

"I'm sorry. I have to take this. It's my brother and he wouldn't call at this time if it wasn't something important. Make yourself comfortable, I won't be a minute," I tell her.

I jump up off the bed, trying to ignore my erection as it presses uncomfortably against my trousers. I can hear Natalie sighing as I leave the room. I pull the door closed behind me.

I know how she feels, but I plan on getting this call over with quickly and then making it up to her.

"What?" I demand as I take the call in the hallway.

"Charming," Matt laughs.

"I'm kind of busy here. What do you want?"

"Well seeing as you brought it up, what I want is for you to stop fucking potential clients Seb. Jeez. Can you not just keep it in your fucking pants for once?"

Apparently I can thanks to him.

"I don't know what you're talking about," I say.

"Sure you don't. This could blow the whole deal," Matt says.

I can hear the irritation in his voice. It should be me who is irritated. I'm the one getting disturbed.

"Don't worry about that bro. The only thing getting blown here tonight will be me. If you ever get off the damned phone that is."

"Do you have to be so crude?"

"Yup."

"Look I get that you think with your cock, but this is an important deal Seb," Matt says.

I'm getting annoyed now. Matt knows I would never do anything that would negatively affect the business.

"Look it's not like I dragged her here kicking and screaming. She made it quite clear she was interested," I say.

"Yeah? And what happens when she finds out you're not interested in anything other than one night with her?"

"Oh trust me. She'll have had that good a time that she won't hold it against me."

Matt sighs loudly.

"Can you just be serious for one moment? You're putting the deal in jeopardy and you know it. And for what? A cheap lay you won't even remember this time next week."

His judgemental tone hits my last nerve.

"You're one to talk Matt. If I remember correctly, and I know I do, it was only a year or so ago that you almost allowed a fucking criminal who was stealing from us to walk free because you started to think with your cock instead of your head."

"That was different," Matt snaps.

"How? Because you were the one fucking up?"

"No. Because Callie wasn't just a conquest to me. I had real feelings for her."

"And how do you know I don't have feelings for Natalie?"

"Do you?"

"Well no, but that's not the point I'm making."

"So what is your point?"

"My point is that I'm perfectly capable of keeping business and pleasure separate. Natalie and I are both adults and this won't affect the deal. Now if you'll excuse me, I've got a horny and pissed off woman waiting for me."

"Wait," Matt says. "There is one other thing."

There's something in the way he says it that piques my
interest and instead of cutting off the call as I had planned to,
I hear myself sigh and ask him what it is.

"Well it's something I know you'll be very interested to hear.
But it's clear you're otherwise engaged so maybe I'll just tell
you later," he teases me.

Now I'm really fucking intrigued. What could Matt know
that he clearly wants so badly to tell me that he's winding me
up this way at one o'clock instead of being in bed with Callie?

"Just spit it out," I say.

"What about Natalie? Isn't she waiting for you?"

Natalie who?

"She can wait another couple of minutes."

"Kimberley is back in town," Matt says.

The playful tone is gone from his voice and I know he's serious. The news hits me like a brick wall and I am momentarily
mute. I find my voice eventually and I croak out a what, but
it's too late. Matt has hung up and I am left with the buzzing
noise of a dead line in my ear.

I freeze on the spot, the phone still glued to my ear although
there's no one on the other end. Kimberley is back in town.
How? Why? When? I have so many questions. I can't believe
Matt dropped that bombshell on me and then hung up. I
finally peel the phone away from my ear, and call Matt, but
the call goes straight to his voicemail. He's turned his phone
off, just like I knew he would.

I curse and throw my cell phone to the ground. Kimberley is
back in town. It plays on a loop in my head as I picture the
girl I once knew. She was stunning with flaming red hair and

piercing green eyes. She had this laugh, a gentle musical sound that was so infectious that anyone around her would automatically laugh with her.

I haven't seen her in like four years, but the vision of her is still as fresh in my mind as it was the day she … Never mind. I'm not going to let myself go there. So Kimberley is back in town? So what?

I hear a door open behind me and I jump. I turn around and see Natalie standing in the doorway to my bedroom. Fuck. I had forgotten she was even here. I can't do this with her. Not now. My erection is long gone, and Natalie won't be the one to bring my cock back to life tonight. I just want her gone.

"Is everything ok?" she purrs.

"Something came up," I say, pleased that my voice comes out even. "I'm sorry, but you're going to have to leave."

"Leave?" she repeats, frowning at me.

She sounds pissed off and I don't blame her, but I can't do anything about it now. I can't bring myself to even look at her, let alone fuck her. Kimberley is back in town.

"Yeah," I say.

She smiles. That seductive smile that a few hours ago, hell a few minutes ago, was driving me wild. Now it only irritates me. Is she deaf or what? Why won't she just go away?

"Or I could wait in your bedroom until you've fixed whatever crisis has come up. I'll keep the bed warm and give you something to look forward to," she says.

She runs her tongue over her lips and I feel nothing.

"For fuck sake Natalie. Take a hint. We're done here. Just get out," I snap.

Her face changes from seductive to shocked and then angry.

"You absolute asshole," she snaps.

She storms back into my bedroom and for a moment, I think she's still not planning to leave, but then I remember her stripping off her trousers. I'm not going to insist she leaves half naked.

I stand in the hallway, still rooted to the spot. I hear Natalie huffing as she grabs her trousers. She comes back into the hallway with them pressed against her front, her shoes dangling from her hand by her side.

I can see tears shining in her eyes. I don't think she's that upset. I think she's angry and humiliated, and I wish I could make it better, I really do, but I can't. Anything I say now is only going to make this worse. I keep my mouth shut as she stalks closer to me.

"You really are a first class fuck boy," she snarls.

I shrug. What is there to say to that? It's not like she's wrong, and it's not like she didn't know that when she came back here with me. She just didn't care when she thought she was going to get her way with me.

I don't say any of that to her. I don't want to argue with her. I just want her gone. I can smell her perfume and now it doesn't smell sweet like I thought it did earlier. It's over powering. Nauseating.

She's still making no move to leave.

"Well? Don't you have anything to say for yourself?" she demands.

"Close the door on your way out," I say.

Her mouth drops open and she shakes her head.

"Wow. Just fucking wow," she says in a low voice that bristles with anger.

She finally starts to walk away from me. She reaches the top of the stairs and turns back to me. I can see the venom in her expression, the embarrassment in her flushed cheeks.

"You should know I don't do business with people who are unreliable. The deal is off Sebastian. Don't bother calling me."

Dammit. That's what Matt said would happen. But then again, he was the one who dropped that bombshell on me. What did he think would happen after that? I have no idea, but I know I have to fix this. I'll give her some sob story, make her feel sorry for me. Maybe I'll even promise to make it up to her at the weekend when my head isn't reeling.

"Kimberley wait," I say, taking a step forwards.

"Did you just call me Kimberley?" Natalie demands.

Fuck. I did. I know I did. There goes any chance I had of rectifying this.

"Natalie," I say, still not quite ready to give up without at least trying to turn the situation around.

"Fuck you," she says.

She starts down the stairs. I hear her running down the hallway at the bottom and then I hear the front door open and slam closed. I don't bother going after her. What's the point? The deal is off. I screwed up big time. And Kimberley is back in town.

I take a step backwards and my back hits the wall. I slowly slide down it and sit on the ground, my knees drawn up and my elbows resting on them. I run my hands over my face and try to make sense of the swirl of bottomless emotions that flood through me.

Kimberley is back in town.

Chapter Two

SEBASTIAN

I've been trying to call Matt for the last hour, but his phone keeps going straight to voicemail. I've called his office and his secretary insisted he was in a meeting. I know that's bullshit. I could hear it in her voice. He's avoiding my calls on purpose.

Well he's not going to be able to avoid me in person. Screw what his secretary has to say. I'm going to have this out with Matt right now. I step out of the elevator and stalk along the corridor. A few associates run back and forth going about their day like the whole world hasn't just been turned upside down. I return their nods, their good morning greetings. It's anything but a good morning, but I remind myself how I let my own emotions screw up a deal last night and I keep myself in control now. I don't want to take my foul mood out on the staff here.

My head is banging from the alcohol last night and the lack of sleep. I was expecting that but I was expecting it to be for a very different reason. The sort of reason that makes the pain bearable.

I move through the open plan centre of the floor, trying to ignore the way the low hubbub of voices pierces my head. Even the sound of computer keys clicking sets my jaw on edge. I reach into my pocket and pull out a strip of painkillers. I dry swallow two and tell myself they're working.

"Rough night?" Bradley, one of our top accountants, grins when he sees me popping the pills.

I bite my tongue to stop myself from snapping at him that it's none of his business. Bradley and I go way back and we've always had an easy relationship, more like friends than a boss and a worker. Any other day I would have laughed and regaled him with stories of the wild night I'd had last night.

"You could say that," I reply, forcing a laugh.

He pulls his desk drawer open and hands me a sealed bottle of ice cold water. I'm glad now I didn't bite his head off.

"Thanks," I say as I open the top and drink half of the bottle down in one go.

The cool water revives me somewhat and I don't know if the pills are kicking in quickly or if I was just dehydrated, but the pain in my head begins to recede, becoming a dull ache rather than a sharp pain. I sit down on the edge of Bradley's desk.

"How's the report coming along?" I ask.

"It's looking good," Bradley says. "I'll have it over to you by the end of today officially, but unofficially, I've been through Benton's books with a fine tooth comb and they're a good investment. They're financially strong, and with a few tweaks, they could be a real cash cow."

I nod thoughtfully. Bradley is right. I knew it from a quick glance over the figures, but I wanted to do due diligence and be certain there were no skeletons lurking in their books before I began the negotiations. They're due to get underway in the next week or so.

I feel better about Natalie suddenly. Her company was small fry compared to Benton's. And if we pull off the Benton merger successfully, no one will give a shit about Natalie. Not even my father.

"Nice work," I say to Bradley who beams under my praise. "Dot the I's and cross the T's and get the report to me by lunch time and take the rest of the day off."

"Thanks Sebastian," he says, clearly taken aback.

I laugh and pat him on the shoulder before moving on towards Matt's office. I feel a little calmer and more in control of myself as I reach Matt's secretary's desk, but I'm still in no mood to be fobbed off.

"Morning Sheila," I say, not stopping.

"Mr Hunter doesn't want to be disturbed," she says, jumping up and standing between me and the office door.

"Ah come on now," I say, giving her my most charming smile. "You know that doesn't include visits from his baby brother."

She blushes a little and smiles.

"Well ummm, let me go check with him," she says.

That's the confirmation I needed that he's not with a client. I side step around her and put my hand on the door handle.

"No need," I grin, slipping inside before she can do anything else to try and stop me.

She hurries in behind me.

"I'm sorry Mr Hunter, I ..."

"It's ok," Matt cuts her off.

"Right. Thank you. And sorry again. Would you like some refreshments?" Sheila stammers.

"No thank you. Sebastian won't be staying," Matt says.

He aims the comment at me. I just smirk at him until Sheila leaves the room pulling the door closed behind her. As the door closes, my smirk fades and I march towards Matt's desk, ready to demand to know why he's dodging my calls. Before I can speak, he looks at me disapprovingly.

"You look tired Seb. Late night last night?" he says.

Everyone is a damned comedian it seems.

"Funny. Why the hell are you dodging my calls?" I demand.

"Because I had nothing to say to you. I owe you none of my time Seb. Your actions last night have caused us to lose a client. Natalie Graham called this morning and made it clear we won't be getting her business."

"And who's fault is that?" I say.

"Umm yours," Matt says, raising an eyebrow.

"Yeah I'm pretty sure I'm not the one who interrupted us with a phone call. Let's just say after that, the mood was kind of ruined."

"I wonder why that was," Matt says.

I ignore the jibe. This is nothing to do with Kimberley. This is about the business.

"You accused me of putting my personal life above the business, and now you're dodging my calls in work time because you're annoyed that I called off a one night stand?"

"I'm annoyed that you put yourself in a position to lose us business," Matt counters.

I shrug and sit down in the seat opposite his.

"Whatever," I say. "Natalie's business was a drop in the ocean compared to the Benton merger. I was calling you to see how close we are to getting the first meetings set up. Bradley has just about finished up the financial report and everything is looking as good as we hoped it would."

"We're almost there. The preliminary talks have gone well and we're looking to get started early next week," Matt says. He grins. "But you know all of that. So why don't you tell me what you really want."

"That was what I really wanted. To call you out on ignoring my calls," I lie.

"Ok, I hear you loud and clear. So if that's it then, I've kind of got work to do," Matt says.

I can tell by the gleam in his eye he knows why I'm really here. I mean sure I was annoyed at him dodging my calls, but he's right. I didn't need to ask about the Benton merger. I knew all of that. And if the meetings got pushed forward, of course someone would have reached out to me and let me know. I'm annoyed at him for dodging my calls because I wanted to ask him about one thing. Her. Kimberley.

I eye Matt as I try to work out a way to bring the conversation around to Kimberley without it being obvious I've thought of nothing but her all damned night. His lips curl up slightly at the corners and I know he's enjoying my discomfort. I suppose this is his pay back for all the times I've embarrassed him over the years with new girlfriends. And for all the flirting I do with his fiancé, Callie.

I don't want to give him the satisfaction of asking him for more details about Kimberley, but I know I can't just get up and walk out of here without hearing everything there is to know about her return. I look down into my lap.

"Is it true what you said last night? Is Kimberley really back in town?" I say.

Matt doesn't answer immediately and I force myself to look up and meet his eye. His amused look pisses me off but I bite my tongue, waiting for an answer.

"It's true," he says.

I feel a mixture of emotions flood me. I'm happy to hear that she's back, and at the same time, I'm apprehensive to know that I might run into her. I am also fuming that she's made no effort to contact me. But then why would she after what happened between us?

"Have you seen her?" I ask.

Matt seems to be determined to make me ask the questions to get the information from him, even though he must know it's killing me to have to practically beg him for the information.

"Yeah I've seen her. I ran into her a couple of days ago. She looks good Seb. Damned good. She still has that shock of red hair; it's right down almost to her ass now. And she's filled out in all of the right places if you get my drift."

Oh I get his drift alright. My cock is twitching just thinking about Kimberley all grown up.

"She's really grown into herself. She's beautiful now," Matt says.

"She was always beautiful," I say before I can stop myself.

Matt grins at my words.

"But then all of the women I sleep with are beautiful," I add, more for my own benefit than his.

If I thought he was going to let me save face that easily, I was sorely mistaken. He is most definitely enjoying my discomfort. He nods, an exaggerated nod.

"Yeah I'm sure they are, but not like Kimberley. She's ... something else," he says.

"Maybe I should be calling up Callie and telling her she's got competition," I say.

Matt laughs.

"I don't think she'd be even close to how jealous you are right now," he says. "About our chat I mean."

"You spoke to her?" I say, again ignoring his jibe.

"Sure," Matt says. "I told you I ran into her. What did you think I did? Just ignored her?"

I shrug. I hadn't thought that for a minute, but I just wanted to find out what they had to talk about without having to come out and ask, but Matt pauses again, clearly waiting for me to ask. God sometimes I really fucking hate Matt. He loves to watch me squirm and today is no exception.

"So how is she? What's she up to?" I ask, doing my best to sound like I'm just making casual conversation.

"You seem awfully interested in her," Matt says.

"She's an old friend. Why wouldn't I be interested in how she's doing?" I ask.

"You weren't interested when I told you I ran into Bobby St Clair a couple of weeks ago."

"Who?"

"Exactly. You don't even remember half of the people you used to know. But Kimberley ..."

"Is different," I finish.

My small confession softens Matt slightly and he begins to tell me about their run in without me having to keep digging for more.

"She's good. She's done well for herself. She's the CFO at a big company. She's in town on business actually. She's staying at the Hilton on Mercer Way. She always did like her luxuries. And now she's living the jetsetter lifestyle. She's just got back from a three month tour of Europe. Rome, Paris, Madrid, Prague. You name it, she's been there."

"Sounds like she's really made it," I say.

"Yeah she has. You should see her tan. She was glowing," Matt adds,

There's one more thing I want to ask, but I am afraid of the answer. I think I know the answer. Kimberley was never really the settling down and getting married type, but people change. I've changed. Maybe she has too. I have to know.

"So does she have any kids?" I ask, skirting around the topic.

"Kimberley the workaholic with a kid? Are you kidding me?" Matt laughs.

Despite myself, I find myself laughing along with him. Nothing about Kimberley says maternal. She never hated children, she just hated the idea of having her own. Being tied to a tiny human instead of a desk was never her idea of a life she wanted.

"It was a dumb question," I admit.

And not at all the one I wanted to ask.

"I wonder how her partner feels about her aversion to kids," I say.

I was going for casual, but I can hear the tremor in my voice as I say it and I know Matt must hear it too.

"She hasn't got a partner currently. And when she finds one, she's not exactly backwards in coming forwards. I'm sure she'll make it known early enough in the relationship that if it's a deal breaker, the guy can flee."

"Yeah," I laugh. "Kimberley doesn't hold back. If she wants something, then everyone knows it. And equally if she doesn't want something then everyone knows it."

Like when she no longer wanted me.

I push the thought aside, concentrating instead on the joy of hearing that she's not taken. Not that it matters. I'm well and truly over Kimberley and I don't want to go back there. Not even a little bit. I was just curious that's all.

I try to convince myself my thoughts are true. It's hard work, but I think if I tell myself it often enough, I can start to believe it. Because no matter what happens, no matter what old feelings hearing Kimberley's name stirs up inside of me, it's in the past. She's in the past. And I won't risk going there again.

I've heard enough and although hearing Kimberley isn't married stirred a warmth inside of me, a warmth I haven't felt for a long time, I know the idea of running into her is dangerous. I stand up abruptly.

"Well I best be getting on. Listen Matt, I'm going to organise a business trip out of town."

"What?" Matt demands.

"You heard me. I don't need a reminder of the past Matt. I'll be going somewhere far away and staying gone until Kimberley goes back to wherever the hell she came from."

Matt jumps up and crosses his office, standing in front of the door so I can't walk out. What is it with people standing in front of doors today?

"Look Seb, I know I've been winding you up about this, but come on. Think rationally. The Benton merger is reliant on you being here and you know it."

I shrug. I'm really past caring right now.

"You're not seriously telling me you're going to leave town and blow a deal this big over some girl are you?" Matt says, an eyebrow raised.

I sigh. He knows exactly which buttons to press in me to get me to come around when it matters. Because he knows as well as I do that I'm not going to do that. I've worked too hard on the preliminary stuff for the merger. I can't just walk away and let it all fall apart now. Losing Natalie's business was one thing, but losing the Benton merger isn't something I can come back from.

"I'll be here," I say. "I was just blowing off steam. Of course I'm not really going to leave town because of Kimberley. Why would I even care if she's back or not?"

"Why indeed," Matt laughs.

It didn't take him long to revert back to winding me up now he knows that he's made it almost impossible for me to leave town and save face. I nod towards the door which he's still blocking.

"Now if you don't mind, some of us do have actual work to get on with," I say.

Matt stands aside with an eloquent hand gesture. I roll my eyes and leave his office. My mind is reeling but I just have to forget about Kimberley, forget about the past, and concentrate on getting through the pile of paperwork on my desk.

My headache is starting to come back and as I approach my office, I ask Bernie, my secretary, to run out and grab me a double shot latte. She smiles and jumps to her feet.

"Do you need anything else while I'm out?" she asks.

Just a one way plane ticket to Outer Mongolia or somewhere equally remote.

"Nope. Just the coffee will be great," I say.

I go into my office and sit down and begin looking over the pile of paperwork in front of me. No matter how much I stare at the rows and columns of figures, I can't get Kimberley out of my mind. I find myself picturing her how she used to look. Sweet faced, young, innocent. I try to imagine her all grown up, her cheeks filled out, her breasts filled out, curves on her hips. I feel my cock starting to get hard just picturing it and I groan to myself. How can she still have this effect on me after four fucking years?

I'm seriously debating going into my bathroom and jerking off, but to do that would be to admit that Kimberley still has that kind of power over me, and I won't allow her any more space in my head. I fire up my computer and force myself to start reading and responding to my emails. Bernie comes in with my coffee and a toffee flavoured donut. I raise an eyebrow at the donut and she laughs.

"I thought maybe you could use the sugar rush," she grins.

"Do I look that rough?" I ask.

"Oh you look terrible," she laughs.

"Good to know my misery amuses you," I say.

"Always," she laughs as she breezes back out of my office.

"You're fired," I shout as the door begins to close.

"Love you too," I hear her reply.

Bernie has been with me since I joined the company straight out of high school and like Bradley, I think of her more as a friend than an employee. It's a running joke between us that unlike most of the other people here, Bernie tells me the truth, even when I won't like it. I then tell her she's fired and she makes some sarcastic little come back.

I must look as rough as I feel for Bernie to feel the need to bring me sugar though. She knows I rarely treat myself to anything sweet. All the same, I pick the donut up and take a big bite. Instantly, the sugar makes me feel better. I finish the donut and lick the sugar from my fingers and then I start on the coffee. As I'm sipping it, my phone rings. I pull it out of my pocket and look at the screen. Chance. My other brother, the middle child.

Great. Has he been having sneaky meetings with Kimberley too that he now wants to rub in my face and gloat about?

"Hey," I say, taking his call. "What's up?"

"Ah not much. Just checking in," he says.

"Checking in?" I repeat. "Is that necessary?"

Jeez can't a guy have a fucking hangover in peace around here?

"Well maybe not, but I thought it wouldn't hurt. Matt told me he told you about running into Kimberley."

Ah so he has called to gloat. It's nothing to do with my hangover. Obviously.

"Yes, he took great delight in dragging out the story of their meeting, so if you don't mind, I'm really not in the mood for round two of that," I say.

"Relax would you? Believe it or not, I have better things to do than wind you up. I just wanted to make sure you were ok. I know the effect she has on you," he says.

God, there's no damned effect. I'm over her.

"I'm fine," I assure Chance. "Matt's had his bit of fun and it's done. It's not like I'm going to run into Kimberley and if I do, then I'll deal with it. It was a long time ago and yes, she used to have an effect on me, but that was then. I'm a grown man now and I'm totally over her."

"Whatever you say bro," Chance replies.

He doesn't sound like he believes me for a second, but at least he doesn't sound amused like Matt did.

"So have you ran into her as well?" I ask.

"No, but I've heard from people other than Matt that she's back," Chance says.

He answers my unasked question. Was Matt full of shit to get his own back on me for blowing the deal with Natalie.

"Honestly Seb, I wouldn't worry about it. It's not like she's exactly going to be going out of her way to see you either is it?" Chance says. "But just on the off chance you do happen to see her at some point, just be cool. Like you said, you've grown up now and so has she. Leave the hurt where it belongs."

"Oh I intend to," I reply.

I sound more determined to do that than I feel. Chance's words hit me hard. I should be glad to realise that Kimberley will be as happy to avoid me as I am to avoid her, but I'm not. The notion causes a lump to form in my stomach. God how did we fuck things up quite so spectacularly?

"Well if you're sure you're ok, I'll let you go. I've got a mountain of paperwork to get through and I've got a couple of meetings lined up this afternoon. And then tonight, I have a dinner booked with a potential new client," Chance says.

"Jeez Chance take a day off. The world won't stop turning you know," I say.

Chance laughs.

"You're funny Seb. I'm glad you haven't lost your sense of humour."

He hangs up before I can explain that it wasn't a joke. Chance is a complete workaholic. Even my father, another workaholic, comments on how much work Chance does and the amount of hours he puts in. Don't get me wrong, I love my job, and I work way more than my fair share of hours, but Chance is on another level. Work is his entire life.

I turn back to my computer, but I already know I'm not in the right frame of mind for this. I knew it the moment I fired the thing up, but I finally allow myself to admit it. I decide to take the advice I gave Chance. I finish my coffee and put the cup in my desk bin and then I stand up and leave the office.

"I'm taking the rest of the day off," I tell Bernie. "Can you reschedule my two o'clock. Hold my calls unless it's to do with the Benton merger."

"Got it," Bernie says. She looks at me critically, assessing me. "You look like you need a day off. Go home and get some sleep. Just looking at you is making me feel tired."

"You know, you're enough to give a guy a complex," I laugh.

"What can I say? Honesty is my middle name," she replies.

"Yeah I get that. Maybe you should aim for tact instead," I say.

"If you wanted tactful, you'd hire a Sheila," she winks.

I can't argue with that any more than I can face another minute in this suddenly too hot building. I throw Bernie a wave and hurry away.

J've spent as little time at the office as I can this last week. In fact, I've spent as little time as I can anywhere but in my own house. I haven't neglected the details of the merger. Everything is coming along nicely and I've been working on the financial side of it all from home. One thing I am sure of is that this is a great investment and I'm not going to let my crankiness affect the deal.

As much as I've tried to tell myself my recent state of apathy has nothing to do with Kimberley, I don't really believe it. I mean I am over her; how could I not be after four years? But her name still has power over me. And I fucking hate that.

I've tried my best to keep her as far away from my mind as possible, so if anything, I've actually gotten through more work than I usually would have. I've not only been working on the Benton merger, I've also been doing some research for our next acquisition and I've found several good candidates. I've spent my so called spare time researching the firms and getting deep into their books.

Kimberley has still been a constant feature in my thoughts the second I step away from my laptop though. As much as I don't want to see her and drag open old wounds, I can't help but wonder why she has made the effort to see both Matt and Chance but not me.

Chance called me last Thursday to tell me that he had spoken to Kimberley. She'd called him and asked him to meet up with her for coffee. While there, she told him she'd grabbed a coffee with Matt too. That irritated me more than anything. Matt had implied him seeing Kimberley had been a chance encounter. I know he kept the rest a secret to save my feelings; even though he enjoyed winding me up, he didn't really want to hurt me, but I still would have liked the truth.

Chance pretty much confirmed what Matt had told me. Kimberley is hotter than ever.

It's such a weird place I find myself in. On the one hand, Kimberley is the last person I want to see. Really. I don't need a reminder of the past. It's not like I could ever really forget it anyway. But at the same time, I'm finding it so fucking hard to function just knowing that she's in town and hasn't made any effort to reach out to me when she had no problems reaching out to both of my brothers.

I know I could call her, but to what end? To have her confirm in person that she doesn't want to see me? She made that much clear by meeting up with my brothers and not sending me so much as a hey how are you text message.

Screw it. Screw her. I have an important meeting today and I can't let her into my head again. Matt wasn't kidding when he said the meetings would be starting early this week. It's only Monday and the first meeting is happening in half an hour. I just want to pop up to my office and grab the last of the files.

I walk along the hallway and when Rachel, the sexy as fuck head of advertising greets me, I give her a quick smile. Her frown tells me I'm off my game. I would normally have had a bit of witty banter for her, a bit of flirtation. Today though, I'm just not in the mood for it.

Maybe it's because I had the worst weekend ever. I shake my head. I haven't had such a rubbish weekend since ... Well suffice to say it's been a long time.

I reach my office. Bernie is sitting at her desk sipping a coffee, another one sitting on the corner of her desk waiting for me. I smile at her and pick it up.

"Look at you in early," she grins.

"I didn't know you were keeping tabs on my time keeping," I snap.

The grin slips from her face.

"I'm sorry," she says. "I was just joking."

God I hate being so fucking cranky. Bernie says shit like that all the time and I just laugh at her.

"No, I'm sorry," I say genuinely meaning it. "I had a crap weekend and I took it out on you."

"What happened like?" she asks.

I sit down on one of the visitor's chairs and glance over my shoulder to make sure there's no one else in hearing distance.

"Nothing happened. That's the problem. I went out for a couple of hours on Friday night and I just wasn't feeling it you know? Saturday, I didn't even bother."

She raises an eyebrow and then she grins.

"So you didn't get laid and now you're pissed," she says.

"Exactly that. You know me so well Bernie," I say.

It wasn't like there hadn't been options. The bar I went to on Friday had been full of hot women. I'd targeted a pretty little brunette, and she was up for a night of fun. She had that air about her. But my heart wasn't in it. I just wasn't in the mood for more mindless sex. I don't think she was too happy when I bailed on her. If only she'd known I wasn't too fucking happy about it myself.

"Are you alright Sebastian?" Bernie asks, pulling me back out of my head. "Seriously. Has something happened? You're ... I don't know. Different."

"I'm just feeling a bit out of sorts. I think maybe the pressure of the Benton merger is getting to me a bit. But I'll snap out of it. Don't you worry about me," I say, forcing a smile.

She doesn't look overly convinced but she lets it go. She knows there's more to it than I'm letting on. There is a lot of pressure surrounding the merger. It can take our empire to the next level, but I thrive on pressure. The higher the stakes, the more I come alive. Bernie knows that. But she also knows that when I'm ready to open up to her, I will do it in my own time, and all the questions in the world won't make me open up any sooner. This time, I really don't think I'll ever be opening up about this.

I just need to hear word that Kimberley's business here is done and that she's gone back to wherever is home for her these days, and then I'll be back on my game. I have to get back on my game now though. I have to hold it all together through this meeting and be charming. I can't go in there biting people's heads off.

I check my watch. I've sat here too long and now I've only got five minutes before the meeting starts. I get to my feet.

"Thanks for the coffee Bernie," I say.

"Any time," she replies, knowing I'm thanking her for more than the coffee.

I go into my office and grab the last few files. I have the most important ones on me, but I don't want to leave myself in a situation where a question might come up that I can't answer without these last few. I leave my office and almost run to the elevator. I go up to the tenth floor, and make my way to the big conference room. I step inside.

The meeting has already started, but a quick scan of the room shows me Matt, Chance, Bradley and several of the associates who will be handling the day to day parts of the merger. I breathe a sigh of relief. The client isn't here yet.

I take my seat and Matt glares at me. I flash him a grin, ignoring his obvious anger.

"What did I miss?" I ask.

"We were just going over the brief one more time," Chance says, pushing a folder towards me. I open it and start flicking through it, double checking everything is in place. "We want to start negotiating this deal from a position of strength and we all need to be on the same page."

He doesn't look as angry as Matt does, but I can hear the strain in his voice as he struggles to not snap at me. I almost comment that if we all need to be on the same page, maybe we should present a united front by not all sniping at each other, but I bite my tongue. We will be having some version of that conversation later on, but not in here in front of the associates.

Hayley, one of the marketing associates saves me from having to say anything else when she pipes up with a question. Matt starts pointing out parts of the report and explaining it to her as I take a more thorough look through the brief. I have seen several drafts of the brief, but I always like to go over every-thing and just make sure it's all exactly as we discussed before starting a meeting.

As I'm treble checking the figures, the door to the confer-ence room opens. I hear it in some far of place in my mind, but I don't full register it. At least not until a voice I would know anywhere follows the closing of the door.

"Hi everyone. I'm so sorry we're late. The traffic out there is crazy this morning."

I feel my whole body stiffen. Every muscle inside of me turns to stone. My heart races, beating so fast I'm certain the whole room will be able to hear it. I try to swallow but my throat is dry. Unlike my palms which are suddenly coated in a layer of sweat.

It's been four years since I heard that voice, but I would still know it anywhere. I could pick out a whisper from that voice in a sea of yelling. It's her. Kimberley.

Suddenly, it all drops into place. The way Matt wound me up about seeing Kimberley. The way Chance lectured me about not letting the hurt in if I should come across her. The way everyone has been extra cagey about revealing any names when it comes to the Benton merger. I didn't press for them. One CFO is the same as the next one to me. I work in numbers, not names. But this CFO is anything but the same as the rest of them. She's supposed to be my past, yet here she is, very firmly planted in my present and my future.

I can hear her voice still as she greets Chance and Matt and the others. Two other voices join in with the introductions, not that Kimberley needs any introduction. She's brought with her the CEO and the VP. So at least my brain is still functioning. It's only my body that seems to have failed me completely. I just can't bring myself to look up from the brief I'm staring at but no longer reading.

"Oh don't worry. He always was thorough," Kimberley says, and I know she's talking about me.

She's excusing my rudeness, no doubt to Matt. I can't just sit here like this. The whole room has gone silent and I can feel every eye on me.

Just breathe. Just act like a normal fucking person.

I look up and all eyes are indeed on me. I force myself to smile. I clear my throat.

"Sorry, I was engrossed there," I say with a fake cheeriness. "Sebastian Hunter. The numbers guy."

The two men with Kimberley introduce themselves. Joe Benton, CEO, and Gary Parker, VP. I nod at them and then I do what I knew I would have to do. I turn to Kimberley. My eyes meet hers. I am once more frozen. The casual greeting I had planned freezes on my lips. Her eyes are exactly as I remember them. Bright green with tiny flecks of gold that seem to dance in the sunlight. The quick glance I had of her before I met her eye told me Matt is right. She has grown up. She has changed a lot. But her eyes have never changed even a little bit.

I know that our gaze is affecting Kimberley almost as much as it's affecting me. I can tell by the way her pupils dilate as she looks at me, the way I hear her let out a small gasp that sounded so loud in the silence of the room.

Someone clears their throat and the moment between Kimberley and I is broken. She looks away and lets out a long breath. A breath she was holding because she too froze when our eyes met.

"How are you Sebastian?" she smiles, gaining her composure a lot quicker than I do.

I still can't speak, and I just nod to her. It's enough to break the spell in the room and the three newcomers take their seats. An awkward silence still hangs over us, and I still feel as though everyone is looking at me. It's as though my whole fucking life has been projected out for the entire room to see.

I finally find my voice and I turn to Chance.

"Want to get this started?" I say.

He nods and begins to talk and the atmosphere in the room melts away. I try to focus on Chance's words, but it's almost impossible for me to look anywhere but at Kimberley. It doesn't matter. I know Chance's spiel almost as well as he does.

I shift uncomfortably in my seat as my cock begins to respond to the vision of beauty sitting across from me. Her breasts have indeed filled out, as have her hips. She's all woman now, there's no denying that. That innocent look she always had is gone, replaced with a quiet inner confidence that radiates out of her, showing her to be a force to be reckoned with.

That's my Kimberley. A force of nature. A force of nature that might just be about to break me once again.

Chapter Four

SEBASTIAN

This damned meeting drags more than any meeting I've ever been in. Hell it drags more than my classes at school used to when all I wanted was for the school day to be over so I could spend time with ... well, her.

Kimberley and the others ask questions; way too many for my liking. No, actually that's not fair. They clearly know their stuff. They ask all of the right questions. All of the questions I would have asked had I been on their side of the table. But it feels like a slew of pointless questions because I have a list of questions of my own. Questions that I can't ask in a meeting. Questions I'll probably never get to ask and never get the answers to.

I want to ask Kimberley a thousand questions. Why she is back. Why now? Why did she choose our firm for the merger when there are hundreds of other firms out there she could have done business with? I mean I get it. We're the best. But she must have known she'd have to face me. Which leads to me more questions; the ones that will really hurt. Does she not care at all about seeing me again? Am I really just a short chapter in her life's book? Why did she ...? No I won't go there. I'm not even going to ask that question in my head. Not now. Not ever.

And I have a ton of questions for Matt and Chance too. How long have they known Kimberley was involved in the merger? Where they talking business when they went for coffee and just forgot to mention that part to me? And why the fuck did they think springing her on me like some unwelcome surprise birthday present in the middle of a meeting like this was a good idea? Did they really think I would just welcome her with open arms? Do they really think I don't have a right to be so damned pissed at her?

I honestly can't believe Matt had the front to lecture me about being unprofessional after what happened with Natalie when all along he knew he was planning on this damned ambush. If he makes even one comment about my conduct in this meeting, I don't think I'll be able to stop myself from punching him. Seriously, what was he expecting to happen here? Why does he enjoy my misery so much? And why did Chance go along with it? Don't they know how much is resting on this deal?

"Sebastian," Bradley hisses, pulling me away from the list of unasked and unanswered questions in my head and back to the meeting, where I've clearly been asked a question I should be able to answer. Perfect.

I take another quick glance at Kimberley. She's poised, confident. She doesn't look the least bit perturbed by us being in this room together. Other than her short gasp when our eyes met, it's like she doesn't even know me. Well two can play that game. It's time to put my game face on.

"I'm sorry," I say, flashing my most charming smile at the three people opposite me. "I tend to zone out through the formalities. The truth is, you know this is a damned good growth opportunity for Benton's. We know the same is true for us. So why don't we cut the bullshit and get down to the real questions."

Joe looks at me for a moment, his expression unreadable. I stand my ground, holding his unwavering gaze. It's a make or break moment for the deal and I should be sweating buckets right about now, but honestly, I'm just glad for the excuse to keep my eyes off Kimberley for a moment. As Joe and I face off against each other, the whole room goes silent. It's that moment where no one dare so much as breath.

Joe's face breaks into a grin and I hear the collective exhale around me. He gives a short laugh.

"I like this guy," he announces. He turns to Kimberley. "Good call to approach the Hunter's with our proposal."

That causes me to raise an eyebrow. So Kimberley has been talking to Joe about me. Or at least about my family. Her cheeks turn the tiniest bit pink and I take a moment to enjoy her discomfort. Call me petty, but it's kind of nice to not be the only one on the back foot here, even if it is only for a fleeting second before Kimberley regains her composure. She gives Joe a warm smile.

"What can I say? I know you hate this dance and I know Sebastian likes to get down to business as much as you do."

So it was me specifically she's been talking about. I'm not keeping score or anything, but if I were, I'd be thinking Sebastian one, Kimberley nil right about now.

"Kimberley is right. I do hate this dance. My time is too precious to waste and I'm sure you all feel the same way about your own time. As Sebastian here said, we all know this merger is a good opportunity for both of our businesses. So how about we stop with the questions we all already know the answers to and move onto the real dealings."

"Works for us," Matt says.

"Good," Joe replies. "Let's arrange a date to exchange our books and get the financial stuff out of the way so we can open the doors to a discussion on how exactly this is all going to work."

Chance opens up his laptop and goes into our calendar app.

"Does tomorrow afternoon work for you?" he asks.

Joe raises an eyebrow and I have to bite my lip to stop myself from smiling. Chance doesn't even bother trying to hide his smile. He's got Joe and he knows it.

"Sorry is that too soon? Just you said you didn't want to mess around and we're prepared to get this thing done as soon as possible."

Joe regains his composure and nods.

"Tomorrow works for us."

I stand up, and again all eyes are on me. Jeez, they're acting like I've just pulled my fucking pants down or something.

"What?" I say, faking innocence. "The meeting is over isn't it? Unless anyone else has any questions that can't be answered in the next stage?"

I pause giving everyone a measured look and a chance to respond. No one speaks up, just like I knew they wouldn't.

Who would dare ask a question at this point when it's clearly on the table that we're past that point? I nod, vindicated and leave the room without a backwards glance.

My abrupt exit isn't just about Kimberley. It's about keeping the power on our side of the table. Waiting to be dismissed from a meeting is the equivalent of saying the other side is in charge and I'm not about to go there. Both Matt and Chance know this is my style, and they know it works. But I can still feel the daggers on my back as I leave the conference room. They think it's all about Kimberley. And they think I'm the one who is obsessed with her. I'm starting to think they're the ones who think everything is about her.

I walk towards the elevator without looking back, aware that I am being watched through the glass wall of the conference room. I pull my cell phone out and put it to my ear. It's not ringing, but it gives me something to do with my hands and it makes it look like I have already moved onto something more important than the meeting I've just left. Another power play.

I reach the elevator and step inside. I put my cell phone back away and press the button for the fifth floor so I can go back to my office. I change my mind as the door pings open and press for the ground floor. I need a cigarette badly.

I hurry through the busy lobby and go around to the side of the building. I lean back against the wall for a moment and take a few deep breaths. It'll be fine. Joe Benton wants this merger as much as we do, and if he wants it, it'll happen. Unless we fuck it up. And we won't, because I am staying firmly away from it from now on. I've showed my face and there's no reason Matt and Chance can't handle the rest of the negotiations. And Bradley can step in for the numbers element.

I pat my jacket pockets and then my pants pockets looking for my cigarettes.

"Fuck," I say when I come up empty.

Of course I don't have any cigarettes on me. I quit like two years ago. I guess Kimberley is having more of an effect on me that I realised. Fuck it. One won't hurt. Maybe even one packet. I've quit once, and I can do it again. Once Kimberley is gone from my life again. Even if the merger is successful, which I know it will be, I can make sure I don't end up in a position where I have to work with her, or see her again.

I head back towards the building. I decide to ask Sheila, Matt's secretary, to run out and grab me a packet of cigarettes. I really don't need the lecture I'll get if I ask Bernie to go. I'm almost back at the elevators when one pings open and Kimberley, Joe and Gary step out.

Dammit.

I turn around quickly and head back for the main doors. I hear Kimberley telling Joe and Gary she'll catch up with them.

Double dammit.

Obviously they saw me. I hoped I had turned away quickly enough, but clearly I haven't. I up my pace, hoping if I just keep my head down and keep going, Kimberley will take the hint and leave me alone. She doesn't of course. Taking a hint never was Kimberley's style. She likes thing straight forward. No mind games, no drama. No hints. Just say what you mean. I thought walking away made my meaning clear enough, but evidently not.

"Sebastian," I hear her calling. "Wait up."

I can hear her heels clicking as she hurries along behind me. I know I can just keep going. She'll never catch up to me in heels. But I also know that she knows there's no way I won't have heard her calling out to me. If I just keep going, she'll know I've done it on purpose to avoid talking to her. And she'll think it's because her presence is getting under my skin.

She's so far under my skin she's practically a part of me, but she doesn't need to know that. I stop walking and take a deep breath and then I slowly turn around to face her.

She's wearing a tight black pencil skirt and a yellow blouse that's open at the collar. It's open enough to suggest that the good stuff is underneath it, but not enough to be unprofessional. Her hips push the skirt out nicely, showing off her shapely waist and her gorgeous curves. Her bright red hair shines like a fucking halo and her eyes hold me under their spell the same way they always have.

The way my cock stands to attention at the mere sight of her isn't just because of our history. There's no denying that she is beautiful, but it's more than that. Kimberley Montgomery is a force to be reckoned with and it shows. Her quiet confidence oozes out of her and she owns any room she walks into.

If she was a stranger who walked past me in a bar, I know for a fact she would capture my attention just as she is now. To be honest, if we didn't have history, I'd be all over that, in a bar, in the office. Fucking anywhere.

She covers the couple of paces that separate us. I force myself to smile.

"Hey Kimberley," I say.

She smiles back at me and I think I see relief in her smile. She thought I was going to be a dick about this. She thinks

I'm still hung up on her. Screw that. I'll show her I couldn't give a flying fuck about her one way or the other.

"It's good to see you Sebastian. How's things?" she asks.

Fantastic until you showed up and reminded me why sex with other women, even smoking hot ones, is almost always unsatisfactory.

Chapter Five

KIMBERLEY

*A*s Joe, Gary and I step out of the elevator and into the crowded lobby, I see him. Sebastian Hunter. It's all I can do not to suck in an audible breath. That guy knows how to rock a suit.

He's changed a lot since I last saw him. His body has filled out. His shoulders are broad, his chest muscular beneath his shirt, and I just know that he has a six pack to die for. He's definitely not the gangly teen I remember. His hair is what I can only describe as city trendy. A tad too long to be a corporate look, revealing the rebellious nature of him. Typical Sebastian. He was never one to follow the rules.

His eyes seem to be darker than I remember them. Beautiful eyes that I could lose myself in if I let myself. His smile hasn't changed a bit though. The way his lips turn up at one corner, the smirk of a man who knows exactly who he is and doesn't give a shit what anyone thinks of that.

It's the sort of smile that turns my knees weak and makes my pussy wet. It makes me wonder what sex with Sebastian would be like now. It makes me think it would be a whole lot better than the fumbling sex we had as teens when neither of us really knew our bodies or what we liked.

He doesn't grace me with that sexy smile now though. Instead, he turns away the second he spots me and begins rushing through the lobby although his intention was always to leave the building, even though he was obviously heading towards the elevators.

Gary and Joe don't seem to notice. Why would they? The lobby is busy enough that one person wouldn't stand out to them. They wouldn't be able to spot Sebastian through a crowd of thousands like I would.

We step out of the elevator and I know I have to go after Sebastian. I have to talk to him. I have to show him that I'm here for business and nothing more. I can't let our history get in the way of this merger. Not when I have worked so hard to get to where I am now. And especially not when I recommended the Hunter's firm as the best option for us.

There's not many twenty-two year olds who can say they're the CFO at one of the top accountancy firms in the city. In fact, there are none except for me. And I'm not about to let the history I share with Sebastian get in the way of that. I need him to know that I plan on handling this in a business like way; and I need to know he can do the same.

Joe has no idea I have history with Sebastian. He knows I know the Hunter family of course. I had to tell him that much to explain how they got on my radar when Joe starting talking about a merger. I know I should have told him about our history, but if I had, he would have pulled me off the deal and sent in someone else. Someone who hadn't put the hours of blood, sweat and tears into the prep work.

I'm not about to stand by and let someone else take my moment.

"I'll catch up with you guys," I say to Joe and Gary.

"Ok," Joe replies. "Meet us back at the hotel. We'll go over the figures one more time and Gary and I will quiz you on anything the Hunter's are likely to spot and question."

"Uh huh," I say, barely listening as I hurry away.

The numbers won't be what throws me off my game. I know numbers. Numbers don't have added depths or unresolved issues. With numbers, what you see is what you get. They don't lie or tell a half a story as long as you know how to read them, and I know how to read numbers a damned sight more than I know how to read people. It won't be the questions that trip me up. If anything, it'll be the person asking them. The person with the warm brown eyes and the smile that can turn me into a melting pot of lust.

I hurry across the lobby after Sebastian, cursing myself for wearing heels. I'll have to call out to him. If he ignores me, then at least I know where I stand and I can prepare for a hostile meeting bubbling with old resentments. It's the last thing I want, but if it comes to that, I can handle it. I've handled meaner guys than Sebastian in my time working for Benton, although none of them have had any sort of personal connection with me. I don't know how I'll fair really if someone who is such a big part of making me the person I am today truly hates me.

"Sebastian. Wait up," I call before I can talk myself out of it.

He stops moving, but he doesn't turn around immediately. I know what's going through his head. He's debating walking away, but he knows if he does that, I'll know that he heard me and chose to ignore my shout. This is the moment I will know for sure exactly how hostile the merger is going to be. If he waits for me, there's hope we can be professional and get through it. And if he doesn't, then at least I'll know to brace myself for a dirty fight instead of a peaceful negotiation.

I keep walking and slowly, Sebastian turns to face me. I feel the knot of tension in my stomach slowly begin to ease up a little. It's still not going to be easy, but it's going to be possible and for that at least, I am grateful.

Sebastian smiles at me as I close the gap between us. I feel my stomach flip and my pussy tighten as I look at him.

Dammit Kimberley, get a fucking grip. This is ancient history. It didn't work out then and it won't work out now. So be professional and nothing more.

"Hey Kimberley," Sebastian says.

His voice is low, husky. And simply hearing him say my name makes my pussy wet. God I need to stop this shit. I'm not some stupid teenager anymore. I'm a grown woman with a real career and I need to start acting like it.

"It's good to see you Sebastian. How's things?" I say.

I'm relieved when my voice comes out sounding normal. I was half expecting it to be croaky or just die in my throat altogether. He doesn't respond. He just stands there looking at me in amusement. What is so fucking amusing about this? Is he enjoying my discomfort? Most likely he is. I try again.

"It's been so long hasn't it?" I say smiling.

He gives me nothing but that amused look in return. Some-how, this is worse than being yelled at or ignored, both of which were potential scenarios I had prepared for. This cocky demeanour was something I hadn't even considered. It's so not the Sebastian I remember. The Sebastian I remember would have done anything for me, at least until I broke his heart. But this new Sebastian? I have no idea how to handle him.

"I've managed to catch up with Matt and Chance since I've been back, and it's good to finally get a chance to catch up with you," I say.

I see Sebastian's face change slightly although he tries to hide it. Is that why he's pissed and acting like this? Because I've seen his brothers and not him? How can he not know why that was? How can he not know that I contacted his brothers because they were the safe options? And surely he knows that I was hoping they'd tell him about our catch ups and that maybe, just maybe, he'd call me and we could just forget about the past and move on.

Now I've seen this side to him though, I'm not sure I'd have wanted him to call me. I really don't have time in my life for this petty nonsense and quite frankly, I'm done trying to play nice with Sebastian if he's just going to stand there looking at me like I'm some animal in a circus doing tricks for him.

"For God's sake Sebastian, are you broken or something?" I snap.

"Or something," he says.

He turns to walk away from me and I am at once pleased that he's finally responded to me and pissed off that he thinks he can just dismiss me this way. He wouldn't act like this around Joe or Gary and I'm as much a part of this damned merger as they are. And Sebastian is either going to have to learn to deal with that, or stand aside and let someone else handle it.

I reach out and touch his upper arm, stopping him from turning away from me. The second I touch him, I feel a spark fly up my arm. Even through his suit jacket I can feel the chemistry sizzling between us. I pull my hand away quickly and clear my throat to cover my sharp intake of air. I don't know if Sebastian felt what I felt when I touched him, but he's stopped trying to walk away which is something.

"Look Sebastian I've tried to meet you half way but you clearly don't want to be friends or whatever and I'm cool with that. But let's get one thing clear here. This is business and I expect you to treat me with the same courtesy as you'd treat any other potential client or partner. Is that clear?"

"Crystal," he responds, that amused expression back on his face.

Is this just the way he looks now? No. He didn't look like this in the meeting. In fact, until the end when he made the kill shot on the discussion, he looked every bit as thrown as I felt.

"We both work on the finance side of our businesses and I can't see any scenario where we won't be working on this merger together. And I'm cool with that. I just want to make sure you are too," I say.

"Of course. It's business Kimberley. I do this shit every day," he says.

He turns and walks away from me again, and this time, I make no move to stop him. I can't help but admire his toned ass as he walks and I instantly reprimand myself and force myself to look away.

Sebastian has made it quite clear I am nothing to him. Nothing except an obstacle to getting the deal he wants out of the merger. I've tried to be friendly and clearly, he doesn't want that. So screw how fucking sexy he is. If he wants the gloves to come off, then mine are well and truly off and we'll do this the hard way.

I've already won this battle. Sebastian might have stopped when I called after him, but he's still given himself away. Instead of heading out of the building like he tried to imply he was doing when he spotted me, he's headed straight back to the elevator.

I'm the one wearing the cocky smile as I move across the lobby and out of the building.

Chapter Six

SEBASTIAN

*I*t's been another long day to say the least. First the meeting from hell, and then the conversation with Kimberley in the lobby. I know I played that awfully, but when it comes to Kimberley I seem to have only two modes. Lose my shit or turn into a complete jerk. I went with the complete jerk option. I stood there looking at her like she was just a side show in the deal and I know that's not fair. But as I discovered at eighteen, life isn't fucking fair.

What I should have done was calmly explained to Kimberley that it hurt me a bit to know she'd contacted my brothers and not me, but that it was water under the bridge and I would work with her and be courteous and professional. Instead, I stood staring at her with a cocky grin and ignored her attempts to extend the olive branch until I finally made it sound like I thought she was the one acting crazy by telling her I do these kinds of deals all day.

Let's just say it was far from my finest hour, but it served a purpose. It convinced me I was doing the right thing handing this over and taking a step back from the negotiations.

I spent the rest of the day holed up in my office craving a
cigarette and going back over Bradley's report with a fine
tooth comb. I needed to make sure every single number was
right, because while I can bluff my way through questions I
don't necessarily have the answers to, I would never expect
Bradley to do that and Bradley is going into that meeting
tomorrow. Him and Kimberley can spend the time going
through each other's books. I trust Bradley to spot any anom-
alies in theirs, and I have no intention of subjecting myself to
another couple of hours in a room with Kimberley.

It's after eleven when I finally leave the office and I want
nothing more than to go home and crash, but I know no
matter how tired I am, I won't be able to sleep until I've had
this out with Matt. If I drop the Bradley thing on him in the
morning, he'll only argue with me and it won't do to have the
whole company seeing us go toe to toe with each other. And I
still want some answers as to why he thought not mentioning
that Kimberley was a part of this merger was a good idea.

I head out to Matt's apartment building and get out of my
car. His doorman recognises me and doesn't question why I
am there. I ride up to Matt's floor and storm into his apartment. Matt is sitting on the couch, his laptop open on his
knee and a glass of wine on the coffee table beside him.
There's no sign of Callie and I figure that's a good thing. She
doesn't need to get pulled into this shit.

Matt looks up and frowns as I storm into his apartment.

"What the hell are you doing here Seb? It's gone one o'clock
in the morning."

"I've just finished work and we have some things to discuss,"
I say.

"I'm kind of tired and I was just finishing up here and going to bed. We'll talk tomorrow," he says.

"No we won't. We'll talk now. Or are you plotting some other fun little game behind my back that you want to spring on me at work in front of everyone?"

"What the hell are you talking about?" Matt snaps.

"Oh come on Matt. Why didn't you tell me Benton's CFO was Kimberley? Did you think it would be fun to drop that little fucking bomb in the middle of a meeting the way you did?"

"I didn't think you'd care. Since when have you ever cared who's on the other side of the fence? What is it you say? Oh that's right. One face inside of a suit is the same as the next one."

"This is different and you know it," I say.

Matt just shrugs.

"Whatever. I should have told you. I'm sorry. Now is that it? Because like I said, I want to go to bed. I've got an early start in the morning."

"Oh I'm sorry the most important merger our company has ever worked on is inconveniencing your beauty sleep," I say.

Matt rolls his eyes. I ignore the gesture.

"Unlike you, I happen to think there are some things that should be done behind closed doors rather than in front of the people who work for us. Which is why I'm here to tell you in person behind closed doors that I won't be in the finance meeting tomorrow. Or any of the other Benton meetings. I've showed my face; Joe Benton knows I'm on board.

Bradley will be handling all the financial stuff from here on in."

Matt jumps to his feet.

"Are you out of your fucking mind Seb?" he shouts.

His face is rapidly going red and the vein in his head that stands out when he's particularly stressed is coming up fast. I was expecting an argument, but I didn't expect this level of a one. I actually thought he would get it, and that he would be relieved to have the loose cannon out of the way.

"Not at all. I just trust Bradley to handle this," I say.

It's not a complete lie. I do trust Bradley, but Matt and I both know I would never pass something so important off to someone else, not even someone I trust, under any normal circumstances. But nothing about these circumstances are normal.

Matt sits back down and sighs loudly.

"Look I trust Bradley too. But not with this. You said it yourself Seb. The Benton merger is the whale. We can't afford to screw this up. You will be in that meeting tomorrow and you will not only go through those books like your life depends on it, but you'll answer any questions Kimberley has about our books properly."

"Wait. Did dad die and no one told me? Because unless that happened, I'm pretty sure you're not the boss and you don't get to call the shots."

"You really want to bring dad into this? You really want me to call him and tell him you can't handle the fucking heat on this thing so you're palming it off to one of our accountants?"

I don't. I should never have mentioned dad. I dread to think what his reaction would be if he knew the extremely thin line I'm walking with Kimberley. I'm not ready to concede yet though.

"Sure. Call him. Why don't you tell him I pulled your pigtails as well?" I rant, pacing up and down in front of Matt where he still sits looking up at me like I'm some animal that needs reigning in.

"Look just take a moment to calm down Seb. I'm not going to call dad and you know it. Just think about this rationally for a moment."

It irritates me no end how Matt can sit there so calmly. It irritates me even more when he tells me to calm down.

"Are you crazy Matt? You seriously think me and Kimberley can work together? After everything that happened between us? Or is there something else you're not telling me?"

"Like what?"

"Oh I don't know. Like you want this merger to fail for some reason and you want someone to blame for it if it does."

"If I wanted the merger to fail, I would have suggested sending Bradley to the meeting instead of you," Matt says quietly.

Touché.

"So what is it then? Do you want everyone to be as miserable as you are?"

Matt actually laughs.

"What makes you think I'm miserable? I've never been happier than I am right now."

"I don't know Matt. I don't know what's going on in your head, but you know as well as I do that this is a bad idea, and yet you're pushing for it anyway. So come on. Tell me what I'm missing here."

"You want the truth? This is the biggest deal we'll ever make or break. And no one knows the figures like you do Seb. The point you're missing is the part where you act like a grown up and separate our business from your personal drama."

"That's rich coming from you," I say. "Your personal drama almost allowed a criminal to walk free."

Matt gets to his feet again. He looks pretty angry now too.

"Yeah you're right. It did. I fucked up and I'm not afraid to admit it. But you were the one who had my life about it. You were the one who insisted that I should have been able to control myself and get the job done."

"So that's what this is. You're punishing me for telling you that you screwed up?"

"What? No. This isn't any sort of punishment or twisted game. You want to know why I didn't tell you Kimberley was the Benton CFO? Because I knew you would over react like this. I thought if we kept it from you until the merger was underway, you'd see that it was too late to back out and that you'd man up and get on with it. Seb we need you on this and you know it."

"I'm not over reacting. I'm taking myself out of a volatile situation that you and Chance created. This isn't just about me Matt. It's about Kimberley as well. Do you honestly think we're the right people to negotiate any sort of deal?"

"Yes," Matt says. "Because Kimberley has assured me she will be professional about this. Benton wants the merger and

Kimberley knows her whole career is riding on getting this right. She's not going to risk messing it up over some shit from the past. I honestly thought you would be able to do the same."

If Matt had come to me and told me all of this before I encountered Kimberley, I would have thought the same. I would have honestly believed I could keep it professional and not let a bunch of old feelings and resentments affect me. But now I'm not so sure I can. How can I get Matt to let this go without admitting that though, because there's no way in hell I'm telling him the truth; that even after all of this time, seeing Kimberley again has thrown me so far off my game I'm afraid I'll never get back on it again.

I sit down heavily on the couch and run my hands over my face. Matt sits down in the chair opposite me. We fall silent for a moment and then Matt breaks the silence.

"Ok, you win. But Bradley is not handling that meeting. Come to my office first thing in the morning and talk me through everything and I'll take the meeting. Clearly you're still as frazzled by Kimberley as you always were and I won't have the fact you're still in love with your high school girl-friend ruin this deal."

"I'm not still in love with Kimberley. That's ridiculous. And I don't get frazzled over any fucking woman. I'm the one who leaves them wanting more, not the other way around."

I am so fucking angry that Matt could even suggest such a thing. As if I'm still in love with a girl who left me four years ago. I mean don't get me wrong, I can admit that she's fucking gorgeous and I could fuck her all night long, but that doesn't mean I'm in love with her. It means that she's nice to look at and nothing more.

Matt raises an eyebrow and watches me as I fight to swallow down my anger. If I bite now, then he'll know he's hit a nerve. I know exactly what he's doing. He's playing to my ego and he's backed me into a corner.

He's left me with two choices. I can suck it up and work with Kimberley, or I can back out and have him think I'm still in love with my ex and that her very presence is enough to throw me off my game.

"Well played bro," I say, smiling despite myself. "I see you've been taking in some of my tricks after all."

Matt smiles and gives me a single nod.

"Nothing like playing to someone's ego is there," he grins.

"You know what? I have nothing to prove here, but if you're so determined to have me work on this merger that you're willing to start using the tricks you claim to disapprove of so much, then screw it. I'm in."

"Perfect," Matt says with a smug smile that tells me he knew this would be the outcome from the moment we started to have this conversation.

"But know this Matt. If this deal ends up fucked up because Kimberley feels like she has something to prove and tries to play hard ball with me, then that's on you."

"Noted. But if you screw this up because you disrespect Kimberley and act like a dick to her to the point where she pulls the plug on the whole thing, then that's very much on you."

Chapter Seven

SEBASTIAN

I glance at my watch. It's fifteen minutes before Kimberley is due to arrive and my heart is racing and my palms are sweating. I jump to my feet and go into my bathroom. I run my hands and wrists under the cold water tap for a few minutes until I feel calmer.

This is starting to really piss me off now. I feel like I'm starring in some rom-com where the prom king asks the geek girl on a date. I'm the teenage girl in this scenario. Like her, I know something will go wrong, but like her, I cling onto the hope it'll all turn out ok in the end. She'll get the guy at the end. And I'll get the merger. Hopefully.

I examine my face in the mirror for a moment. I expect to see bags underneath my eyes, my cheeks sunken in and a grey tinge to my skin. But I look normal. Like Kimberley isn't having any effect on me. That's something I suppose. I loosen my tie a little bit and nod my head in satisfaction. The slightly more casual look will let her know I'm not in the least bit worried about this.

"Don't you dare fuck this up," I say to myself in the mirror.

I leave the bathroom to find Bernie coming into my office.

"Everything ok?" I ask her.

I want her to say no. Something major has come up. Something only you can fix, and you have to leave right now. Of course she doesn't.

"Yeah. I just popped in to tell you Kimberley Montgomery is here for your meeting," she says.

Of course Kimberley is early. As if Little Miss Corporate would be anything but efficient.

"Thanks Bernie. Let her in. And can you grab us some coffee?"

"Sure," she says. She smirks. "She's very pretty."

I need to nip any ideas Bernie has of acting as my wing man in the bud right now.

"Been there done that Bernie, and it was nothing special," I say.

Bernie's jaw drops and then she gives a low whistle.

"Oh my God. You're in love with her aren't you? Is that why you've been acting so strange lately?"

"What? I'm not in love with her," I say. "I wish everyone would stop saying that. And I haven't been acting strange."

"Whatever you say," she grins as she walks away from me.

Why the hell does everyone think I'm in love with Kimberley? I mean I know people say there's a fine line between love and hate, but this is getting ridiculous now. I don't even hate her. I just strongly dislike her. And Bernie doesn't even know

I have history with her. Is there something in the water at this firm or what?

I open my mouth to say something else and then I close it again. If I keep adding on more and more reasons why Bernie is miles out of left field, then she'll start saying I'm protesting too much.

Bernie goes back out of my office and I move to the window. I take a moment to look out at the view of the city. This is our fucking city, our empire, and I won't let Kimberley, or more likely the way she makes me feel, ruin it for me.

I hear my office door open and I know without turning around that it's her. I smell her scent. Vanilla and something else beneath it. Something primal. I swallow hard and look at her reflection in the glass. She stands uncertainly between the now closed door and my desk. Good. I'm glad she's fucking nervous. It makes me feel slightly better to know I'm not the only one who is way out of their comfort zone here.

I take a deep breath and turn around. I give her my corporate smile, the one I use to charm potential clients and investors. Not the one I use on people I like. Not my real smile.

"How are you Kimberley?" I say, stepping towards her and extending my hand.

She gives me a shy smile and slips her hand into mine. I feel it instantly. The same thing I felt when she touched my arm in the lobby yesterday. It's like her hand is too hot and it sends fire through my whole body. The sort of fire that could consume me if I let it. But I won't let it. I won't even entertain the notion of it.

I shake her hand firmly and then drop my hand to my side, suddenly unsure of what the hell to do with it. It hangs limply for a moment and then I indicate the chair in front of my desk.

"Take a seat. Bernie's grabbing us some coffee and then we can get started," I say.

Kimberley sits down and crosses her legs and I can't help but notice how her skirt creeps up an inch before she pulls it back down.

Why Kimberley, are you trying to seduce me? I shake my head and look away. Of course she isn't trying to seduce me. I'm not really in a movie, and certainly not that one. She's just getting herself comfortable.

I go around my desk and sit down in my chair. Bernie enters right on cue and I want to jump up and hug her for her perfect timing, but that would be weird all round so of course I don't. Instead I thank her like a normal person and pick up my coffee. I take a sip which obviously burns my lip but I don't show it. I put the cup back down and look at Kimberley again.

God why is this so fucking hard? I have zero issues making small talk normally, but how do you make small talk with someone you used to know without crossing the line from professional to personal?

"Are you ready to get started?" Kimberley asks.

She sounds confident, forceful even, but I think I detect a slight note of uncertainty in her voice. This is clearly as awkward for her as it is for me. Maybe even more so after my ridiculous performance in the lobby yesterday.

"Yup," I say.

Yup. Not yes, or sure, or any of a hundred normal responses. I go for yup. Real smooth Sebastian.

I open my top drawer as Kimberley brings her briefcase up onto my desk and opens it. She pulls out a thick file and I pull out a matching one from my desk drawer. Kimberley puts her briefcase on the ground beside her feet, beside those fuck me heels she's wearing, and slides the file over to me. I take it from her, nodding my thanks, being careful not to let my fingers brush against hers. I wonder if she felt the same fiery feeling as I did when we shook hands earlier. Probably not.

I push my file towards her and we both open the files at the same time and begin looking through them. The one she gives me is pretty standard and nothing jumps out at me as being wrong and no funds seem to be unaccounted for.

I am very much aware of Kimberley's presence as she flicks through my file, tapping a red nail on the desk. Her tapping is something she's always done when she's concentrating and the memory brings up another wash of resentment that fills my throat like bile. I force myself to swallow it down. I promised myself I wasn't going to screw this up. I won't let Kimberley get to me.

"Where is ...?" Kimberley starts.

I hold up one finger and cut her off mid-sentence. Why the hell did I do that? God I'm such a fucking douchebag when I'm not in control of a situation. I pretend to really focus hard on the figures in front of me for a moment and then I glance up.

She still has one perfectly in place eyebrow raised when I look up. I flash her a quick grin that I hope will ease the tension, but the look on her face tells me it didn't work.

"Sorry," I bark. "I just thought we should both go through everything and save any questions for the end."

"Whatever Sebastian," she says with a sigh.

I risk another glance up at her after a moment has passed. She's back to focusing on the folder in front of her and I allow myself to relax a little bit again. The crisis has been averted. She hasn't bolted for the door and ran to tell Matt she can't possibly work with me. I can still pull this back.

I continue on with the file, forcing myself to lose myself in the numbers. They're good. Very good. And it's clear to me that Kimberley is very good at her job. There isn't a single thing I can question in the figures. That's probably a good thing. The less conversation we have to have, the less chance there is of me saying something stupid and blowing things up between us. The less time she is here in my office, the less chance there is of me reaching out and tucking the loose strand of her hair behind her ear and stroking her porcelain smooth looking cheek.

What? Why am I even considering doing that? I look back down at the file quickly, losing myself in the figures, a place of safety and very much my comfort zone.

I finish looking over the accounts and I quietly close the folder and take a sip of my coffee while I wait for Kimberley to finish up. Is she just being thorough or is she going to have a list of complaints that will be completely unfounded? I think of earlier when she tried to ask me something. It started with where is and then I cut her off. Where is what? There's nothing missing from the file, of that I am certain, and if she starts making accusations of me hiding anything from her, then she'll be out of the door. End of. Matt can moan all he likes but I don't do business with people who accuse me of anything underhanded.

She finishes reading through the file and closes it. She looks up and nods her head.

"It all looks to be in order," she says.

Did something she saw after speaking answer her question or has she actually found something and plans to use it against me later? I should let her. There's nothing off in that file, I know it with a certainty that's beyond anything I've ever felt before. I made damned sure everything was perfect for this. She will make herself look so stupid if she questions me in front of her boss and I shoot her down.

But that's not how to start a good business relationship and I remind myself yet again that I promised myself I would do this right and treat Kimberley like any other potential associate. And if it was anyone else, I would give them the chance to ask their question privately.

"It is," I say. "You were going to ask me something earlier though."

"Oh. Yes," she says. "I was going to ask you where the bathroom is."

"Oh," I say feeling like the biggest jerk in the world for making her wait until we'd finished going through the files to ask that. I point to the door behind me. "It's back there. Or if you're not comfortable using that one, there's a ladies' room by the elevator."

"Thanks," she says.

She gets up and heads for my private bathroom. I can't help but watch the muscles in her calves move as she walks and the way her hips sway from side to side. She goes into the bathroom and closes the door behind her. I pull my eyes away and run my hands over my face.

Ok this could be going better, but it could be going worse as well. Just tell her everything looks good at her end as well and then tell her you'll be in touch. Keep cool, keep professional. It's almost over.

Kimberley comes back out of the bathroom, interrupting my pep talk with myself. She sits back down.

"So do you have any questions or issues with our books?" she asks.

I shake my head and force another smile.

"No, it's all good," I say. "I'll talk to Matt and Chance later on today and let them know we're good to go on this end."

"Perfect," Kimberley says. "I'll do the same with Joe and Gary."

"Great. Say by five? Then I can give Joe a call and set up a meeting with him and Gary to get the ball rolling on the next stage of the negotiations."

"Just Joe and Gary?" Kimberley says, raising that perfect little eyebrow again.

Actually, I meant the four of us, but the ice cold tone she uses when she thinks she's been excluded gets under my skin again. Why didn't she just clarify it without making it sound like an accusation? I really can't be doing with having to keep dealing with her, and as CFO, her part in this really is over. The rest of the negotiations can take place with or without her, and if she's going to be difficult, then without her works perfectly well for me.

"Well yeah. They're the ones who make the decisions aren't they? You've done your part Kimberley. Go back to the hotel and give yourself a pat on the back and have a spa day or something."

Jeez what the actual fuck am I playing at? If someone had implied to me that my part in a deal was over because the numbers were done, I'd have hit the roof, yet here I am playing that card with Kimberley.

Kimberley stands up abruptly and scoops up the file off the desk. She bends down and picks up her briefcase but she doesn't wait around to put the file inside of it. She heads for my office door without a word, and I have to bite my tongue to stop myself from calling after her and apologising. I can't apologise, because then she'll know I'm being a dick to her on purpose, that this isn't my usual way of handling this kind of deal. She'll know she's getting under my skin, and I can't let her know that or she can play on it in future negotiations.

She reaches out for the door handle. Her hand is resting on it, then suddenly, it isn't any more. She whirls back to face me, her face cloudy with barely concealed anger. She comes back towards me, a lioness closing in on her prey.

Chapter Eight

KIMBERLEY

I am absolutely seething as I make my way out of Sebastian's office. I don't know who the fuck he thinks he is, but he doesn't get to decide for Joe who does or doesn't represent Benton's in a meeting. What an absolute arrogant jerk he has turned into.

I wanted to say something, but I bit my tongue. I'm not going to get into a slanging match with Sebastian. He's not worth the effort. Instead, I'll feed back this information to Joe and make it known I want to be at that meeting. He won't exclude me. Will he?

He might if he thinks bringing me along will be a deal breaker. Well fuck that. I'm not having Sebastian think he is somehow my boss. That won't be the case after the merger, and it certainly isn't the case now. How dare he try to cut me out of my own deal? Who exactly does he think he is?

I turn back to him before I leave the office. He's watching me with the damned smirk on his face again.

I walk towards his desk, trying my best to bite back the anger I can feel. I don't want this to turn into a he said she said style slanging match. I just want to make it clear to him that I will be in that meeting. I want him to think it's going to happen either way and let him think he should just save himself the embarrassment of telling Joe to exclude me. Just in case Joe actually does it.

I reach the desk and bend slightly at the waist, flattening my palms on the desk to keep me from flapping my hands around as I tend to do when I get angry.

"What exactly is your problem Sebastian? Is it because I'm a woman? Or is it more personal than that?" I demand.

He gets to his feet, not wanting me looking down on him for this. I straighten up and stand tall, facing him, looking him directly in the eye. I force myself to keep my hands by my sides and keep them still. It takes everything I have not to ball them into fists, but if I do that, I don't think I'll be able to stop myself from punching Sebastian in his smug mouth.

"I don't have a problem. The finances are covered. What more is there to say?" Sebastian says. "You're being ridiculous Kimberley."

He sounds calm and I sound angry. Great. The hysterical woman cliché is always a treat. I force myself to calm down, counting to three in my head before I speak again.

"I'm being ridiculous?" I repeat with a bitter sounding laugh that I don't like at all. "You're the one being ridiculous. Not to mention childish. Honestly, it's like trying to do business with a sulky teenager."

"I ...," he starts, but I'm not finished and I don't let him cut me off this time.

"Tell me honestly if at any time through your whole career you've tried to exclude the finance team from another company from a meeting," I demand.

He doesn't reply and he won't meet my eye. He shuffles uncomfortably and gives an awkward shrug.

"Yeah. That's what I thought," I snap. "Now I'm going to give you the benefit of the doubt and assume this isn't because I'm a woman."

He does look up then.

"Some of our best associates are women. Don't even try to play the sexism card on me," he says.

"Oh I'm not. I know this is personal. Are you really going to mess this merger up because of something that happened between us when we were just kids?" I say. I pause for a second and go on, some of the anger leaving my voice now. "Do you really still hold a grudge against me for wanting a career of my own? You of all people should understand being ambitious Sebastian. We used to talk about our futures all of the time. And when we did, we always talked about our careers. You knew I wanted more than being some part time shop assistant who lived off her husband."

He looks up and meets my eye. He gives me a sad smile.

"Yeah. I remember. But I'm not the one who shattered the dream. I'm not the one who left," he says.

He doesn't sound bitter or angry. He sounds hurt. Am I imagining this, or is Sebastian still hurt because I left him? Is he acting out because I hurt him and he doesn't know how to act around me?

Surely not. Surely after all of these years he's over it. We were just kids. Kids with dreams and talk of the future. And when we talked of the future, we were always together in it. But things change. How many people actually stay with their childhood sweetheart?

I look into Sebastian's eyes, searching for the answers, but the moment of vulnerability is gone and his eyes are as cold as ice as he looks back at me. Maybe I imagined it after all. Yes, that's what happened. He's just trying to manipulate me, to make me feel bad for him so I excuse his behaviour. And I almost fell for it.

"Look Sebastian, I have no idea what's going on with you or why you're being so hostile towards me, but listen up. It ends right here, right now. I'm as invested in this merger as Joe and Gary. Hell it was my damned proposal. So if you think you can push me aside because you think we're done here, then you're wrong."

"I get it. It's not nice to be pushed aside is it?" Sebastian says.

There's no hurt in his voice this time. There's not even anger. He's back to that look and tone of amusement. He's fucking taunting me, trying to make me bite. Well I'm not going to. I ignore his comment and go on.

"I'm going to be in that meeting Sebastian and you know it. Unless of course you want to explain to Joe that you think I should be excluded from it because I was mean to you in high school. I mean I don't fancy your chances of getting him to take you seriously with that one, but if you want to give it a shot, knock yourself out."

I don't wait for a reply or even a reaction. I just turn and walk out, slamming the door behind me.

"Is everything alright Ms Montgomery?" Sebastian's secretary says as I breeze past her.

"Everything is just perfect," I say.

I am barely out of sight of her desk when I hear Sebastian's office door open. His secretary going in to make his booboo go away? Who knows, who cares. I just hope she can get him to act like a grown up for the rest of this merger which I am regretting more and more every damned day I am here.

Chapter Nine

SEBASTIAN

he restaurant is too hot and stuffy. No it isn't. The restaurant is perfect. Just I am too hot and I feel like I'm trapped in a cage with a wild animal. It's the first time I've spoken to Kimberley since her low parting shot yesterday and quite frankly, she's the last person I want to spend my Friday evening with. She did have a point though. It was never my call who Joe Benton wanted to bring to this meeting, and I would have needed a damned good reason if I insisted on him leaving Kimberley behind. As much as I hate her for what she said, she was right. The reason would have had to been a bit more sophisticated than saying I don't like her because of something that happened when we were kids.

The starters are done and Sasha brings us our main courses, pausing for a moment to exchange pleasantries with me before fading back into the background.

"I have to say the food here is excellent," Gary says as he tucks into his steak.

"So it should be. This place is Matt's baby," I explain.

"He owns it?" Gary asks.

"We own it. But the restaurant side of the business is Matt's area. He's always loved food and the social side of eating," I say. "La Trattoria is our flagship restaurant."

"Throw in a couple of free dinners at this place and it's a done deal," Joe laughs.

"Done," I reply with a grin.

The formalities are mostly out of the way now and this dinner is about more than discussing the finer points of the deal. It's about getting to know each other in a less formal setting, to see if we can gel enough to work alongside each other. I decide it's time to have a little fun. I might not have been able to insist Kimberley got left behind, but I can make her squirm a little.

I turn to her now with an innocent smile, ignoring the way her hair shines, the way her blue dress brings out the beauty of her eyes making them look more intense than ever.

"Do you remember the first time you met my parents Kimberley? Matt cooked dinner for us all," I say.

She smiles and nods, throwing me a warning look.

"I remember," she says guardedly.

I turn to Joe and Gary.

"Kimberley was going through her vegetarian phase," I say. "So she had Matt make her something different to what the rest of us were eating. Ever the gracious host, Matt rose to the challenge."

"Sebastian, they don't want to hear this," Kimberley says through gritted teeth.

"Sure we do," Joe says.

"She was a little nervous about meeting my dad. She wanted to quiz him about getting started in finance, but she was so scared to talk to him. She thought a bit of Dutch courage was in order. Now bear in mind we were like what? Fifteen?"

Kimberley nods, begging me with her eyes not to do this.

"So a couple of beers had quite the effect on her. She slurred her way through her questions and then promptly threw up after eating. She couldn't admit that she'd been drinking, so she said the sauce must have been off. Poor Matt was mortified," I laugh.

Joe and Gary laugh along with me. Kimberley's face is beaming red, but she fakes a laugh.

"I did tell Matt the truth later on that night and he saw the funny side," I add. "What was it he called you?"

Kimberley looks down at her plate.

"I don't remember," she says.

"Oh sure you do. He called you it for like a year until you broke down in tears and begged him to stop. He felt pretty bad about it then."

"I said I don't remember," she says through gritted teeth. She looks up from her plate, glaring daggers at me. "Actually, there was something I wanted to ask you. About the deal."

Sebastian one, Kimberley nil. Or should that be Sickly Kimberley nil?

"Go ahead," I say.

"Where will my office be?" she asks.

"Maybe next to the bathroom," Joe jokes.

"As we said, we've added an extra two floors to our lease for the Benton staff. So I guess wherever Joe puts you," I say.

"I was just thinking I kind of like your office. Maybe we should add a clause in the deal that says I get it," she says.

"Or maybe you should stick to numbers," I smile.

"Ah come on Sebastian. You want this deal. Let me have your office," she says.

"I don't think so," I reply.

"What if I said it was a deal breaker?" she says.

"Then I'd probably say that wine is going to your head," I laugh.

Joe and Gary are both giving Kimberley daggers. She fakes a breezy smile.

"I'm just kidding," she says. "I know Sebastian likes things to never change."

"I think that's called being decisive. Unlike you, I can make my mind up and stick to it."

"So can I. My mind is made up. I'm taking your office or the deal is off," Kimberley says.

"I guess the deal is off then. That's a shame after you put so much thought into your negotiating skills," I say.

I can practically see the steam coming from Joe's ears now and I turn back to him and Gary.

"I think someone's had a tad too much wine," I grin. "She always gets like this when she doesn't get her own way."

"I just think it would show that you're really willing to work as a team player," Kimberley says.

"Yeah? I'm pretty sure the actual merger shows that," I say.

I can see Kimberley squirming. She wants a way out of this conversation, but she's too stubborn to backtrack.

"Also, I noticed in the contract there was a clause to say that Benton staff won't be allowed to make changes to the restaurant side of the business. Why is that?" Kimberley asks.

Oh Kimberley, do you really want so desperately out of this conversation that you're making this worse for yourself?

"Kimberley, enough," Joe hisses, trying to keep a smile on his face. "You know why."

"Yeah. Because Sebastian here can't let go of anything," she says.

"Actually, as I said only moments ago if you bothered to listen, the restaurants are Matt's babies," I point out. "And the clause was discussed and agreed on before it was written in to the contract. Do try to keep up."

"Oh I'm keeping up just fine. But it seems prudent to question the logic of the clause. I mean what's next? What will you try and cut us out of next?"

"Seeing as it was your CEO's idea to put it in the contract, then maybe you should be careful about questioning the logic of it," I say.

"I'll drink to that," Joe says loudly, glaring at Kimberley again.

She raises her glass and awkwardly clinks it against Joe's.

"You know what?" I say. "It seems like you guys still have a few things to discuss. Would you excuse me for a moment?"

I get up and leave the table and head for the bathroom. Part of me is rejoicing at just how far that went. I know Kimberley. Give her enough rope and she'll for sure hang herself rather than admit she doesn't quite know what to do with the length. I also feel kind of shitty. I'm acting unprofessional and I know it. In my defence though I did tell Kimberley to stay away from this meeting. I didn't really think it would go this far. I thought Kimberley would squirm and be a bit embarrassed. I didn't expect her to start trying to change the deal to get back at me. That fuck up is all on her.

I go to the bathroom and stand there long enough for it to be convincing that I've left the table for anything other than to let the sparks become a flame. I step back out and I hear Joe's voice in the hallway. I slip into the staff's break room, leaving the door open a crack.

"What the hell was that Kimberley?" Joe demands.

"I ...," she starts.

"You know what? Don't even answer that," Joe cuts her off. "Get your shit together and start acting like the CFO of Benton's instead of some dumb kid. So Sebastian told an embarrassing story about you? Big deal. It happens when you work with people who know you well. You want to get your own back? You tell a story about him, not start throwing around ridiculous demands and blowing up the deal."

"I'm sorry," she says meekly.

It's a voice I've never heard Kimberley use before and I feel kind of bad.

"This whole thing was your idea Kimberley and you told me you could handle it. Against my better judgement, I went along with it because I trusted you. And now you seem like you're hell bent on blowing this whole thing up. I don't know what's gotten into you, but if you screw this up, then you're done. Am I making myself clear?"

"Perfectly," she says.

I hear them walking away and I shake my head. I've gone too far. I wanted to make Kimberley squirm, but I didn't want it to go far enough that her career is being threatened. I don't like Kimberley. I'd go as far as to say I hate her for what she did to me, but I can't push her to the point where she loses everything. I'm not that guy and I won't become that guy.

I leave the break room and head back to the table, determined to fix this mess. An idea comes to me as I sit back down and note the icy cold atmosphere around the table.

"Did she tell you then?" I grin, acting as though I don't notice the awkwardness.

"Tell me what?" Joe asks.

"I'll take that as a no," I say.

I grin at Kimberley, a friendly grin that I hope she reads as an apology, because it's the closest she'll get to one.

"I can't believe you didn't come clean as soon as I left the table," I laugh.

She looks confused, but she laughs along with me, clearly wondering where the hell I'm going with this, but staying on her best behaviour after Joe's dressing down of her.

"I apologise," I say to Joe, giving him my most charming smile. "We probably took it too far. Past the point where you saw the funny side. The danger of working with old friends I guess."

I turn back to Kimberley.

"Let's just stop messing around now before Joe here has an aneurism and get back to the proper deal."

"Wait. This was a joke?" Joe demands.

I laugh and nod my head.

"Of course it was. As if a pro like Kimberley is going to blow up a merger based on the office she gets," I laugh. "I must admit though, I didn't see the restaurant thing coming. Nice improvising."

Joe and Gary look at each other, and for a moment, the tension around the table intensifies.

"I'm not sure we want to work with people who don't take this seriously Gary. What do you think?" Joe says.

Gary nods solemnly.

"I'm inclined to agree," he says.

Ok, this is going south quickly. I glance at Kimberley who looks almost ghost white. She gives me a look that says fix it. I open my mouth to speak, but before I do, Joe bursts into laughter.

"We had you there didn't we?" he laughs. "You're not the only ones who can have a bit of fun you know."

I laugh with them and Kimberley joins us. There's a shaky quality to her laugh as she plays along as though we set this whole thing up.

"That was a risky little game," Joe says to me. "How did you know I would take it as a joke?"

"I told you him you had a good sense of humour," Kimberley jumps in.

"Ah you know me so well," Joe laughs. "Now, just to clarify, the restaurant clause stays in. And Kimberley? You're getting the worst office I can find."

The mood around the table lightens and by the time Sasha brings us our desserts, we're no longer talking about the idea the merger may or may not happen. We're actively making plans for future projects.

We finish desserts and rather than ordering coffee, Joe orders two bottles of good champagne. He proposes a toast to a great working relationship and we all drink to it.

"So you two obviously know each other pretty well then," Joe says, nodding at me and Kimberley. "Did she tell you about her first day at Benton's Sebastian?"

I shake my head.

"We kind of lost touch after high school," I say.

"Then you're going to love this," Joe says.

Kimberley blushes and shakes her head, but she's laughing and when Joe looks at her, she gives him a subtle nod, letting him know he can tell me the story.

"She came to us as this quiet, shy little thing, but she had ambition. I took her under my wing and yes, I take full credit for the woman she is today," Joe laughs.

I don't think that's entirely true. I reckon I should get at least part of the credit for that one, but that's an observation I keep to myself.

"She walked into my office on her first day as an intern in our finance department. She looks me straight in the eye and says that she's not here to mess around. She tells me that she expects to be CFO within three years and she asks me what she needs to do to get there. Can you imagine it Sebastian? This kid straight out of high school telling me she's here to take over the whole finance department? It took everything I had not to laugh out loud, but she had this quiet determination, and I didn't want to kill her spirit. I told her what I expected, not thinking for a second she'd do it. And yet here we are."

"I can imagine that," I laugh. "Kimberley always knew exactly what she wanted and she wasn't afraid to go after her dreams."

"Knowing what I know about her now, I'm only surprised she came to me instead of attempting to fire the CFO I had at the time," Joe laughs.

"Hey, I'm still here you know," Kimberley laughs. "And let's be honest. If I'd done that I'd have been doing you a favour."

"That's true," Joe concedes.

Kimberley drains her glass.

"Should we order another bottle of wine?" she says.

"None for me thanks. I think I'm about ready to call it a night," Gary says.

"Yeah, me too," Joe agrees.

"Oh, ok," Kimberley says.

"Don't let us stop you," Joe says. "Stay on a while and have a catch up with Sebastian. Just no cooking up anymore tricks between the two of you, you hear me?"

"No, it's fine if you want to call it a night," Kimberley says.

"Nonsense. Stay, I insist," Joe says. "Don't think I don't know you've been dying for us two to leave for the last half hour."

"Huh?" Kimberley says.

"Oh come on. You think we can't see the chemistry between you two?" Joe laughs. "Stay and enjoy yourself."

"There's no chemistry," Kimberley and I say at the same time.

Joe just laughs.

"There's no need to deny it. I like that you two click together. It will help the merger too run smoothly," he says.

He stands up.

"Thank you for a pleasant night Sebastian. We must do it again some time and the next one's on me."

I stand up and shake Joe's hand and then Gary's who has also got to his feet. Kimberley looks like she isn't really sure what to do. She must know that I don't want to spend longer in her company than I have to, but at the same time, after Joe's comment, I understand that she can't insist on leaving.

I sit back down and we watch Joe and Gary leaving in silence. When they're out of sight, I wave Sasha over and ask her for the bill.

"You still pay in your own restaurant?" Kimberley says.

"Sure. It keeps the books right," I say.

She looks at me like she's debating whether or not to say what's on her mind and then she makes her mind up and speaks.

"What changed?" she asks.

"What do you mean?" I snap.

Is she implying I wouldn't usually be professional?

"You were happy to drag me over the coals through dinner and then something changed. What was it?"

If I tell her I heard Joe chastising her, she'll get all defensive and the last thing I want right now is a slanging match with her in one of our restaurants. I decide to go with a half truth.

"I realised I was being a dick," I say.

"Thanks for giving me a way out," she says quietly.

I just shrug. Sasha appears with the bill at that moment and I give her my card. She hurries off to run it through.

"You know Sebastian, I didn't realise how good you are at what you do until tonight. You had Joe practically eating out of your hand," she says. "It's funny because I remember how reluctant you were to join the family business. You were so sure you'd hate it, and yet you seem to be in your element here."

"I am," I agree.

I meet her eye for the first time tonight, letting myself be enchanted by her eyes for a moment. I smile at her, and I know my smile is genuine this time.

"You're pretty good at what you do yourself. I mean you recognised that we were a good asset," I tease her.

She laughs and shakes her head.

"A compliment? I think you might be the one who has had too much wine tonight," she says, but she looks pleased.

"You know something? I don't reckon either of us have had enough wine yet. And I think we deserve another glass or two to celebrate a job well done. What do you say? A drink at the bar before we leave?"

Kimberley looks like she wants to say yes, but something is stopping her, and suddenly, I realise I don't want her to go.

"You know you have to stay out a while in case Joe catches you coming back too early. You might as well have a drink as walk the streets."

She smiles.

"When you put it like that, how can I refuse?"

Sasha brings my card back and we go through to the bar. I order two glasses of white wine and we take a small table beside the bar. I raise my glass.

"To Hunter Benton," I say.

"I think you mean Benton Hunter," she grins.

I raise an eyebrow and she laughs. A warm, genuine laugh that I try my best to ignore. I also try to ignore the way her laugh sends a shiver down my spine. The way my eyes are drawn to her lips.

"Relax, I'm kidding," she says. She clinks her glass against mine. "To Hunter Benton."

We drink and I sit back in my seat.

"So catch me up on all things Kimberley," I say. "How did you end up working for Joe?"

She begins to tell me how she left our city and went down south in search of an internship at one of the big financial companies. She soon learned that without a degree, it wasn't going to happen. She ended up at Benton's when it was a small company, but even then, she could see the potential. She grew with the firm, and now both the firm and Kimberley are a force to be reckoned with in the financial world.

"And now the prodigal daughter returns," I say.

"Something like that," she agrees. "We've talked about a merger before, but Joe has never found a company he liked or trusted enough to go through with it. I've debated mentioning you guys before, but I always stopped myself."

"Why?" I ask.

"It sounds stupid when I say it out loud, but I guess coming home after all of these years, it felt like a step backwards. But this time, it felt right. And it's not a step backwards. It's a step I needed to take. I know I don't have to prove myself to anyone except myself, and maybe Joe, but I have to admit it feels good to come back and show everyone who ever doubted me that they were wrong."

"I don't think anyone ever doubted that you would make something of your life Kimberley," I say.

She smiles and looks down at her glass for a moment.

"Maybe not. Maybe that was all in my head. I guess deep down there was a part of me that was worried I would fail. It was easier to convince myself other people thought I would fail than to accept there was a part of me believed that."

I nod my head.

"I get it. I think that's why I was so reluctant to join the family business. My parents worked hard to build their empire, and Matt joined the company and found his passion. My dad was so proud of him. I wanted that. But there was a part of me that was afraid I would disappoint him. It was easier to tell myself I didn't want to join the business than it was to pull myself up and do the hard miles."

"What a pair of screw ups we were," Kimberley laughs.

I smile at her, shocked that I've opened up to her. I've never told anyone that before, not even Bernie and I tell her pretty much everything. Maybe I have had too much wine after all. It doesn't stop me from getting up and going to the bar for another two though.

"So how long are you staying here?" I ask Kimberley as I sit back down and push her drink towards her.

She picks it up and takes a sip, her eyes meeting mine over the top of the glass.

"For as long as it takes to get what I want," she says after a pause.

I have no idea what she means by that, and I want to press her for an answer, but I stop myself. Maybe it's best to just take each day as it comes.

"So what is it that you want?" I ask.

"Oh I think you know the answer to that one," she says.

She smiles seductively at me and I feel my cock twitching. I swallow hard. She can't mean ...

"World domination of course," she says with a laugh.

I laugh with her. I am equally relieved and disappointed that she was only playing around. Of course she didn't mean me. I am imagining the sparks of chemistry flying between us. I must be. I mean I hate the woman. I'm just letting Joe's earlier insinuation get into my head that's all.

She starts talking again, reminding me of the time she came away for the weekend with my family and we ended up getting lost. We laugh and reminisce about the weekend and about the amount of trouble we got into when my parents finally found us.

"You know, to this day they still don't believe we didn't lose them on purpose," I laugh.

As I talk, my eyes keep going down, drawn to the neckline of Kimberley's dress. She fiddles with a pendant that hangs between her breasts, knowing it will draw my attention and I don't want to let her down. I swear her neckline is lower than it was when we started dinner. I feel myself leaning in closer to her as she admits to me that maybe my parents were right.

"What do you mean?" I ask, my eyes still glued to Kimberley's chest.

Her full breasts jiggle slightly as she laughs and I picture myself ripping her dress away and sucking on her nipples.

"I might have had an idea that we were getting separated from them. I wanted to be alone with you," she says.

She's still fiddling with her pendant, keeping my eyes glued to her chest. She moves her hand slightly and pulls at her dress. Her neckline drops a little further and I swallow hard.

When Kimberley clears her throat, I realise she's stopped talking and I'm just sitting here like a mute idiot staring at her chest. I might as well be drooling down my chin. I drag my eyes back up to her face and she grins.

"You always were easily distracted," she says.

"What do you mean by that?" I ask, still clinging to the hope she hadn't noticed where my attention had been focused a second ago.

"I mean you always were a perv," she laughs.

"I didn't hear you complaining then," I tell her.

"I'm not complaining now," she smiles.

I clear my throat, shocked by her words, and even more shocked to find that I'm happy to hear them. I straighten up in my seat, pulling back from her slightly. I take a long drink from my glass. Kimberley watches me, her eyes full of amusement, a half smile playing across her lips.

"I can't help but wonder what you get up to with women these days," she purrs. "With that charming smile and the magnetism you have."

I know she's playing to my ego, but I play along.

"You think I'm charming?" I say, grinning at her.

I swear I hear her take in a sharp breath when I smile at her. She always used to say my smile would be the death of her.

"You know I do. Your smile has always been my weakness," she says.

"You've always been my weakness," I say.

Shit. What the fuck did I go and say that for? And where did it even come from? I don't even fucking like her.

I clear my throat awkwardly, suddenly looking anywhere but at her. She laughs, enjoying my discomfort.

"You know, I almost forgot how clumsy you could be around me," she says. "I remember now though. How long did it take you to ask me out even after I'd made it clear I was into you?"

I shrug, still not really looking at her. Fucking hell Sebastian, get it together. You're not a daft kid anymore. Seducing women is your thing and you've never been clumsy about it since Kimberley left.

"You used to say it was sweet," I laugh, back in control of myself now.

"It was," she confirms. "But I thought you were all grown up now and that clumsiness was behind you."

I look her in the eye, holding her gaze with mine until I see her cheeks flushing red. I smile again, knowing by the way she shifts slightly in her chair that I'm having an effect on her.

I pull my eyes from hers and move my gaze to her lips. She nibbles her lower lip as I sweep my eyes down to her chest and then back up to her eyes.

"Believe me when I say there is nothing clumsy about me now," I say in a voice so low she has to lean in to hear me.

Her lips are slightly parted, her cheeks still pink. The flush spreads down her neck and over her chest and her neckline is even lower than I remembered it. If she pulls it any lower, her nipples will be out. The thought makes my cock hard and I look at Kimberley, seeing the lust I feel swallowing me whole reflected in the way she's barely breathing as she looks at me.

She sits back slightly and smiles at me. She lifts her glass and downs the rest of her wine, never taking her eyes off me the whole time. A tiny bit of wine dribbles down her chin and I know without any trace of a doubt that she planned it that way. She wipes the drip onto her finger and puts the finger between her lips. I suck in a breath as she licks over her finger tip.

I stand up so quickly I'm surprised the chair doesn't topple over, but it stays upright. I offer my hand to Kimberley.

"You want to get out of here?" I wink.

She nods wordlessly and slips her hand into mine. I can feel the sparks flying up my whole arm as I lead her across the bar and into the dark, cool night.

Chapter Ten

KIMBERLEY

*M*y whole body is on fire as I let Sebastian lead me across the bar and out onto the street. My pussy is so wet I can feel my panties clinging to me. That smile. That goddamned smile I was so determined to ignore.

I don't know how Sebastian has done it, but in the space of tonight, he's gone from almost getting me fired and wanting to murder him, to making me look good in front of my boss and making me want to fuck him until I'm raw.

I promised myself I wouldn't let this happen, but his charm, his smile, the way he looks at me. It all added up and I just can't help myself around him. It will be different this time though. We're adults now. We can make this work. I know we can.

We're barely out of the restaurant when Sebastian tugs my hand and pulls me into an alleyway that runs alongside the restaurant. I don't have time to debate whether or not it's a good idea anymore. Sebastian's mouth is on mine and I can no longer think about anything except how good it feels to finally kiss him again, how right it feels.

My lips respond to his as he pushes his tongue into my mouth. His hands are all over me, moving up and down my body, caressing my hips, my sides, my back. He pushes his hands into my hair, pulling my face tighter against his. I move my tongue against his, tasting wine and chocolate and Sebastian. The taste I remember like it was only yesterday we last kissed.

I can hardly breathe as I am consumed by lust, my whole body is on fire as Sebastian kisses me like he never wants to let me go again. I run my hands down his back, cupping his ass and pressing my body against his. I can feel his hard cock against my stomach and I need more of it. I need to take him in my hands, my mouth, my dripping wet pussy.

I move my hands around to the front of Sebastian's body, taking a half step back but not breaking our kiss. I open his belt and his trousers, digging down inside of his underwear and getting rewarded with his huge cock, already hard as lead and ready for me.

I wrap my hand around it, moving it up and down. I feel him suck in a breath and he lets it out in a moan. He moves his mouth from mine, kissing down my neck. I throw my head back, enjoying the sensation that floods through me as he runs his tongue over the skin and then gently nips me between his teeth.

His hands come to my breasts, roughly kneading them through my dress. I'm not wearing a bra and I know he can feel how hard my nipples are as he skims his thumbs over them, pressing my dress against them and sending sparks down through my stomach to my already clenching pussy.

I up the speed of my hand, working his cock, loving how it makes his breathing change. He twists one of my nipples between his thumb and fingers, sending a shock through my body and making me call out his name.

He roughly grabs my wrist and pulls my hand away from his cock. My eyes fly open, and I find myself looking into his eyes. I can see the lust in his eyes as they seem to darken a shade and the way his lips are slightly parted as he pants. He holds my gaze for a moment, and then he makes a low growling sound in the back of his throat. I move closer, wanting to kiss him again, but he pushes me away, pressing me roughly against the wall behind me, and gets to his knees before me.

He pushes my dress up around my hips and pushes my panties to one side. I hear the tearing of fabric but I don't care. He can rip them clean off me if that's what he wants. My pussy is ready for him, my clit throbbing. My whole body is tensed up, waiting for his touch, silently begging for the release only he can bring me.

He leans in and his tongue is between my lips, seeking out my clit. I can't stop myself from moaning his name as he presses his tongue onto my clit. The throbbing intensifies, sending a screaming need through my whole body. He reaches up, putting one hand on my hip and with the other hand, he pushes two fingers inside of my pussy as his tongue swirls over my clit.

My pussy clenches, pulling him in further, deeper. My hips sway, moving in time with his pumping fingers, giving me more pressure against my clit. I can feel my orgasm building quickly, a deep heat that starts in my pussy and my stomach and spreads out across my whole body. I can feel my muscles clenching, preparing themselves for the pleasure that's about to rip through me.

It's painful to breath now, each breath makes my already erect nipples rub across my dress, teasing me and tantalising me. Sebastian's tongue is working at a frenzied pace, bringing me closer and closer to my orgasm. My hands are balled into fists, one of them squeezing my clutch bag so tightly I'm sure it will break something inside of it.

As Sebastian presses down on my g-spot, I hear myself moaning louder and I bring my bag to my mouth, biting down on it to stop myself from screaming out loud. Sebastian keeps working on me, rough and fast, and there is nothing clumsy about him now. He knows how to make my body sing.

He sucks my clit into his mouth and bites down on it hard enough to hurt. I gasp as pain ripples through me, turning into pleasure as he flicks his tongue over the spot he has bitten. He bites down again, and my orgasm is no longer threatening. It's coursing through my body as Sebastian claims my clit, making me dance to his tune. I can feel my nerve endings standing to attention as fire assaults them. The pain of Sebastian holding my clit in his teeth, stretching it out is over rode by the pleasure of him working my g-spot. I feel a rush of warm heat in my pussy as I gush liquid fire.

I suck in a shuddering breath, holding it, my eyes half closed as the sensations consume me, turning my muscles to jelly. As my orgasm starts to recede, I bring my bag back down to my side. My arms and legs are shaking as Sebastian gets back to his feet with that grin that sends a shockwave through my body. I can see my juices glistening on his face, the moonlight reflecting in the moisture.

I am panting for breath as Sebastian looks at me. His own chest heaves as his pants match mine. I can smell his lust coming off him and the scent of him almost pushes me over the edge again.

I reach out for him and he catches my wrists. He spins me and pulls me back against him. He runs his tongue up my neck again, his hands all over my body, running up and down it, concentrating on my breasts. I can hear myself whimpering as the need for him to be inside of me consumes my every thought.

"Sebastian, please," I beg, my voice breaking.

I don't have to ask him twice. His hands leave my body long enough to push his trousers and underwear down. He pushes against my shoulders and I bend at the waist, pressing my palms against the wall.

Sebastian pushes my dress up around my waist again. He runs his finger through my slit, spreading my juices around. He moans when he feels how wet for him I am, how ready for this I am.

I feel the tip of his cock pressing against my pussy and I side step with one foot, opening myself up to him, inviting him to impale me. He pushes himself inside of me and my pussy opens to accommodate him. He's so much bigger than I remember and I gasp as he slams into me, filling me with his cock.

He begins to move his hips as he grips mine to hold me in place. He slams into me, making me take his full length with each thrust. My pussy stretches, taking him, welcoming the stinging sweetness that he brings to me.

He thrusts, long, fast thrusts that make me cry out each time he enters me. My body is already responding to him, my hips moving despite his hands pinning them in place. I can feel him on every inch of my walls and as he slams off my cervix with each pounding thrust.

He moves his hands from my hips and I feel his hand bunch into a fist in my hair. He yanks it, pulling me upright, making my scalp scream. The stinging turns to pleasure as it moves through my body, the pain feels like ecstasy as he runs his other hand over my hip and stomach.

I lean back against him and he releases my hair, pushing my head to the side so he can kiss my neck.

"I fucking hate you Kimberley," he whispers, his breath tickling my neck and sending goose bumps scurrying over my skin.

His words are at odds with the lust dripping from his voice, from the way he moves his hand lower. He kisses my neck as his probing fingers find my clit. They work in time with his thrusting. He moves quickly now, short strokes that set my pussy on fire. I clench around him, my muscles tightening and he moans against my neck.

"You ruined me," he whispers. "And I'll never forgive you."

He kisses my neck between each word. I turn my head and wrap my arm around his head, pulling him down until our lips meet in a fiery kiss filled with passion. Past resentments fade as we come together as one, a blurring movement of relief as our bodies once more move together.

He keeps working my clit as he kisses me and then he moves his face from mine, running his tongue down my neck again. He nips the skin between his teeth and at the same time, he presses down on my clit. My orgasm explodes through my body, leaving me able to do nothing but make little gasping sounds as I fight to get air into my lungs.

My muscles stiffen, my pussy clenching so tightly I can feel every vein in Sebastian's cock. My back arches, pressing my head against Sebastian's shoulder, my ass grinding tighter into his body as my middle moves away from him.

My pussy throbs pleasure through my body, my stomach clenches in time with the throbbing. All I can think of is Sebastian. I see his face before me, his lopsided smile burning into my brain and I gasp in a breath. I can feel the scream building inside of me, and only Sebastian's hand clamping over my mouth keeps me from releasing it.

He pumps into me as I shake in his arms, my orgasm holding me firmly in its grip. I feel Sebastian's cock twitch inside of me, I hear his sharp intake of breath. His warm seed fills me, spreading its warmth through my body. He wraps his arm around my waist, holding me tightly against him as he spurts again.

He says my name in a gruff whisper. He relaxes his hold on me and his cock slips out of me. We are both panting. I am suddenly conscious of the fact we are in public and I reach up and pull my dress down. I go to take a step away from Sebastian, but he catches me and I spin to face him. His arms are around my waist. I reach up and wrap my arms around his neck, smiling up at him. I pull him closer, resting my cheek on his shoulder, enjoying the way his arms hold me, pulling me against his body. I can feel his chest heaving as he fights to get himself back under control.

"I miss you Sebastian," I whisper.

I didn't mean to say it out loud. It was just a lone thought in my head, but his hold on me tightens for a moment and I know he heard me. He kisses my hair, breathing in my scent and then he gently releases me.

"Let's get you a cab," he says.

It's not exactly the reply I was looking for, but it was a risk saying it at all and his tone is gentle. It's not like he's telling me to fuck off or anything. The disappointment inside of me that he didn't to admit to the same thing is crushing though, and honestly? He might as well have.

"I can get my own cab," I say, a little more snappy than I would have liked to have sounded.

Sebastian just smiles and shakes his head.

"Just because you can do something doesn't mean you should," he says.

I don't want to end up arguing with him. Not after what's just happened between us so I force myself to smile and I nod my head. We slip out of the alley, hopefully unnoticed and I resist the urge to make sure my dress is down. I know it is, and if anyone does spot us coming out of the alley, maybe they'll think we took a short cut or something. If I start pulling at my clothes, I might as well just announce to the world I've been fucked in an alley.

Sebastian steps to the curb and puts his hand out when a cab comes into sight. It pulls up to the curb and he opens the back door.

"Thank you," I say.

"Any time," he winks.

I don't think he's talking about the cab. I'm not and hope he isn't either. I give him a quick kiss on the cheek and get into the cab. I tell the driver where I'm going and I watch in through the back window as Sebastian gets smaller as we drive away. It takes everything I have not to tell the cab driver to turn around.

*F*uck. What the hell have I done? I hate Kimberley and yet I've just fucked her. And the worst thing about it all was that it was good. She was good. It felt right, like I've just been waiting for her to come back into my life so I could claim her as my own once more. But I can't let that happen. I can't let myself feel the feelings that are swirling around inside of me. I have to focus on the pain she caused, the hatred of her that I have held onto for so long. But God was she good.

I run my hands over my face as her cab pulls out of sight. I pull my hands away quickly. I can still smell her pussy on my fingers. It's not just my fingers. Her scent lingers over my whole body like she has marked me as part of her territory. Well not this time. This time, I'm going to be the one calling the shots. And that is not going to happen again.

We're adults now with separate lives and I know Kimberley knows as well as I do that what just happened is a one off thing.

I put my hand out again when another cab appears. I get in and open my mouth to give the driver my address, but instead, I hear myself giving him Matt's address. I don't correct myself.

I pay the cab driver and enter Matt's building. I go to his apartment with no idea of why I'm going there or what I'm hoping to achieve by dropping in on him at this time. I reach out and open his door anyway.

Matt is sitting on the couch, but he's not alone. Callie is straddling him, kissing him. His hands roam up and down her back. She hears me entering and she jumps off Matt.

Shit. Bad timing.

"I'm sorry," I say. "I didn't mean to interrupt."

I turn to leave but Matt stops me.

"Seb wait. What's up?" he says.

I turn back slowly.

"Who said anything was up?"

Matt raises an eyebrow.

"You burst in here at the worst times and normally you're only too quick to tease me and outstay your welcome. But you apologised and went to leave. Something is wrong. Tell me what it is."

I sigh loudly and move closer to Matt and Callie. I flop down on the couch opposite them.

"I had sex with Kimberley," I say.

"Really? That's what you came to tell us? Bravo Sebastian, you got laid," Callie says. "So what's new?"

"Oh you didn't," Matt says.

I nod.

"Can someone please tell me why this news," Callie says.

"Remember when I told you Sebastian is the way he is because he got his heart broken?" Matt says.

I sit up straight and frown.

"I didn't get my heart broken, and what exactly do you mean by the way he is?" I say.

Matt laughs and ignores me.

"Kimberley is the girl who broke his heart," he finishes.

Callie looks at me in surprise.

"She didn't break my heart. I'm the way I am because of my natural charm," I insist.

One look at her face tells me she isn't buying it one bit.

"Ok, fine. She broke my heart. But I was just a kid then," I say.

Callie smiles at me sympathetically.

"Getting your heart broken is the worst feeling in the world isn't it?" she says.

I nod cautiously, not sure where she's going with this. I remind myself she's not Matt and she's not going to make some cheap shot to enjoy my misery.

"I don't get why you're so upset though. I mean you're both older now. Surely having sex with a girl you clearly have feelings for is a good thing right?" she says.

"I don't have feelings for Kimberley," I say. "Well except hatred and resentment."

"Right," Callie smiles. "I get it now. Having sex with her sure showed her."

I groan and bury my face in my hands, ignoring the lingering scent of Kimberley on my fingers.

"So here's the thing," I say, focusing on Callie rather than Matt. "She told me she misses me. I've waited so long to hear those words. To be able to rub them in her face and laugh at her for throwing me away like fucking trash. To tell her it's my turn to break her heart and walk away from her."

"Only now you can't because of the merger?" Callie says.

I could just agree with her. Make out I've come here for a pep talk off Matt about not blowing the deal. The way she's looking at me though, like she actually cares, tells me she deserves more than a lie.

"Only I couldn't because it's not fucking true. It took everything I had not to tell her I missed her too. I didn't know I felt that way until she said it, and then it hit me like a fucking hurricane. It's been four years and I still miss her. How pathetic is that?"

"Pretty pathetic," Matt says with a laugh.

Callie elbows him and shakes her head.

"It's not pathetic at all Sebastian. We can't help who we fall for."

"Clearly," I smirk, looking at Matt. "Or you wouldn't even be here."

I wait for a dig back from Matt and when one doesn't come, I risk looking at him, risk the amusement being written all over his face. It isn't there. Instead, he looks concerned.

"You know what? I'm going to go make some coffee," he says.

He walks over to the kitchen area of his apartment.

"I always knew you were still hung up on Kimberley," he says as he puts the coffee on. "But I guess I thought seeing her again would make you realise it was a thing of the past and allow you to move on."

"That's exactly what I would have thought would happen too. But I don't know. Even after all this time, she just has this effect on me. Like I'm different when I'm with her. I turn into a horrible, snarky dick head. But if I let myself get past that, I'm happier when I'm with her than at literally any other time."

I groan loudly.

"I've done it again haven't I? I've let her get under my skin."

Callie gives me a sympathetic look.

"Maybe she feels the same. She did say she'd missed you," she says.

"No," I say. "Kimberley isn't the settling down type. She's married to the job. She might have missed the sex, maybe even the laughs we had, and for a moment, she let herself believe she had missed us. But deep down, she knows she's not up for any more than a one night stand."

"I don't mean to be rude, but she doesn't sound like a very nice person," Callie says.

Matt laughs.

"She's actually very sweet. You'd like her. She's ambitious, but she's not the kind to go around leading men on and then breaking their hearts," he says.

He comes back over with three steaming mugs of coffee which he places on the table between us. I pick a mug up and sip it as Callie shakes her head.

"It sure sounds like that's what she's done to Sebastian," she says.

"It's not like that," I say. "I haven't exactly given her any reason to believe I had feelings for her. In fact, I've gone out of my way to be a massive dick to her. I just can't seem to help myself. I have two modes round Kimberley. Lap dog or guard dog. So yeah, she has no reason to think I was interested in anything other than a quick fuck for old times' sake."

"So what happens now? Are you going to tell her how you feel?" Callie asks me.

"Nothing happens now. I go back to my life and she goes back to hers. And no, I'm not going to tell her I missed her, because what's the point? What happened between us happened and now it's over and done with. And that's that."

"So you're going to go back to being a dick with her and blow this whole merger?" Matt says.

"Do you have to make this about work? Can't you see your brother's upset," Callie says.

"It is about work," I say gently. "And that's all it can ever be about. I'm not upset, not really. It's just the wine talking. I should have stuck to bourbon."

Callie doesn't look convinced and I turn to Matt before she can say anything else.

"And in answer to your question, no I'm not. I'm going to be professional and so is she," I say.

"Look if it's going to be a problem for you, I can talk to Joe and have him send Kimberley back to her old office a bit quicker than expected. I'll come up with something," Matt says.

I shake my head quickly.

"No. Don't do that. She'll know it's got something to do with me. Really, I'm fine. I've had some sort of epiphany moment or whatever you want to call it. I've finally let myself accept I missed Kimberley and yeah, I guess that's why I have commitment issues. And now I have to finally let her go. And I think I can do that much easier if I just stay out of her life rather than arrange her career for her."

"Ok, whatever," Matt says. "But ..."

"Yeah yeah I know. Don't let it get in the way of work and all that," I say.

"Actually, I was going to say if you change your mind, let me know," he says.

I stand up.

"Thanks bro, but I won't. And I think I've taken up enough of your time now. Callie, I'm sorry for barging in here and interrupting your fun."

"It's fine," she smiles.

"Yeah well I don't want to be the only one getting laid tonight," I say to her with a wink as I leave the apartment.

I can be professional. I can. I've missed Kimberley for four years. What's another few months until this is all done and the dust settles and Kimberley goes back to her life?

Chapter Twelve

SEBASTIAN

I must admit I feel pretty damned pleased with myself as I head back along the hallway to my office. I've just come from Matt's office where myself, Matt, Chance, Joe, Gary and both our solicitor and Benton's solicitor all signed the paperwork to agree to the merger deal. I don't want to sound big headed, but I know how much work I put into this, and I know it's more my deal than anyone else's. Chance even admitted as much after the others had gone when he poured out three glasses of bourbon and toasted to me. Matt drank to me as well, and I although I then felt obliged to return the gesture, it was clear that my brothers were proud of the way I'd handled the talks.

Joe informed us he will be sticking around for a while, around two or three months he reckons, to get his offices set up and his staff settled in smoothly. Once he leaves, he will leave behind some of his key players to oversee the day to day running of it all as well as the administration staff needed to work on our mutual projects. It's pretty much how we expected it to work, and when Joe asked if we had any objections or questions, no one did.

Actually that's not true. I did. I had a huge question. But I didn't ask it. My question was simple. Would Kimberley be one of the key players who stayed behind? I didn't ask it for two reasons. Firstly, I was afraid of the answer. A yes would be bad; there would be the constant risk of me running into her. A no would be just as bad; it would mean there was no chance I would ever bump into her.

See why I didn't ask? It sounds nuts doesn't it?

The other reason was that I wasn't convinced I could ask the question casually. While Joe seemed to find the perceived attraction between Kimberley and I cute, my brothers would have never let me live it down if I'd asked about her in a meeting in any context other than a financial one.

Still though, I'm not going to let Kimberley ruin this moment for me. It's what we've all been working towards for months and the last few weeks have been particularly intense and now it's all paid off.

All in all, I've had a pretty good long weekend. On Friday I had a nice meal in good company and finally got some closure with Kimberley. I spent the weekend thinking about what I said to Matt and Callie. That I missed her too. And I've accepted that was true, and now I know I can move on. I can finally let Kimberley go and move on with my life without her in my head constantly. And then the merger being completed today. How's that for the perfect ending to a good weekend and the perfect start to the new week?

This set up is going to mean a lot of work ironing out the teething problems, but that doesn't worry me. I like to be kept busy, and this is a good step forward for us. Bring it on I say.

I'm almost back at my office when I hear my name being called. I turn to find Matt behind me.

"Where the hell do you think you're going?" he demands.

He looks pretty pissed considering he should be ecstatic.

"My office," I say. "Why? Where's the fire?"

His face breaks into a grin.

"Screw that. Dad just called. He's taking me, you and Chance for drinks to celebrate. He says it's to celebrate the merger. I think it's to celebrate us pulling this off without killing each other," Matt laughs. "Come on. We can start the hard slog tomorrow."

"Sounds good. Let me just go and grab my stuff," I say. "I'll meet you in the lobby in five."

The day only got better after that. Dad was in good form, regaling us with tales of his younger days when he first started out in business and congratulating us over and over again. He told us all how proud he was of us too. We didn't stay out too late; Matt wasn't kidding when he said the hard slog will start tomorrow, and I don't think any of us wanted to face that with a hangover.

I am home by nine. I go through to my bedroom to change, but in the end, I decide to sit in bed and answer emails. There's no harm in getting a head start on tomorrow's stuff and it's not like I have anything better to do. I'd only veg out and watch a movie. I've been sitting here answering various messages for about half an hour when my phone rings. I pick it up.

My stomach flips when I see Kimberley's name on the screen. I sit staring at her name, the phone vibrating in my hand. Should I take her call? What if she's telling me she's leaving? What if she's telling me she's staying?

I ignore the call, letting it go to voicemail. At least then I'll have an idea of what she wants before I have to talk to her. I can prepare myself and have my answers ready so she can't catch me off guard and leave me a stuttering wreck.

The phone stops ringing, but she doesn't leave a message. I put it back down, now more curious than ever about what she wanted that she didn't feel she could leave on my voicemail. I push the thoughts away and go back to my laptop. It's much harder to concentrate now, but I force myself to focus on what I'm doing. Until my phone pings again, this time signalling that I have a text message. It's a relief in a way. I can answer a text message much easier than a call. I can think about exactly what I want to say and rewrite it as many times as I need to so I can get it just right. Jeez it's like I'm that awkward high school kid again. This has to stop. And it will. Right after I deal with this message.

I pick my phone back up and read the message:

"Can we meet up?"

Well that's not what I was expecting. I'm not sure what I was expecting, but I know it wasn't that. I want so badly to reply saying yes. I could ask her to come over now. I've got some wine in the fridge and we could just relax and chat a bit.

I know I can't do that though. Being with Kimberley changes me and makes me crazy. I'd be more likely to invite her over and act like a total dick and berate her until she left, angry with me.

Yeah, it's fair to say I would only end up doing or saying something stupid. It's better that we just leave things like we did. That was a nice goodbye. I debate ignoring the text, but then she'll just assume that I haven't gotten it yet and keep trying. What can I send back that's not a cold, outright rejection but still gets the message across?

I think for a moment and then type out a reply.

"No need. Take whichever office you want."

I look at it for a moment, trying to work out if the jokey tone comes across or if it sounds cold. I decide it sounds cold and I add a smiley face to the end of it. I don't know if that really makes it any better, but it's the best I've got in me right now and I hit send before I can change my mind.

I wait for a reply, my laptop still open on my knee but now ignored. I'm no longer even pretending I can concentrate on replying to my work messages. I wait and wait and after half an hour has passed, I start to relax. She's not going to push for more.

Unless … No, she wouldn't just come over unannounced. She would have no idea whether I was even in. I decide straight away that if my buzzer goes, I'm not answering the door. Then she'll think I'm out and that's why I've blew her off.

I spend the next half an hour with my palms sweating and my heart racing, just waiting for the bell to ring. Once half an hour has passed with no bell ringing, I begin to relax again. I've blown it out of all proportion. Kimberley isn't some crazy stalker type who is just going to turn up at my door unannounced. She's far too cool and in control of herself for that.

I switch off my laptop and decide to get an early night. I'm done over thinking everything. I reach out and put my laptop on the ground beside my bed and then I turn the lamp off. I'm so fucking sick of this. Kimberley is affecting my every waking thought and now I've got her out of my system, I need to get her out of my head, out of my life. I decide it will be a good thing if she is leaving.

~

"So as you can see, this really is the best all round solution for your business needs," I finish.

I've just been talking to a new potential client, George Hayes, through the way our finance department handles expenditure account work and trying to explain to him why we're the best fit for him. George is lapping it up because he knows I'm right. He admitted that he's been to a few other firms and none of them could do exactly what he wanted. We can. It's that simple.

He smiles at me and nods his head.

"I really think ..." he starts.

He trails off as shouting fills my office.

"I've told you he's with a client," I hear Bernie yelling. "You can't just barge in there."

"And who exactly is going to stop me?" a voice replies.

Kimberley. Fuck. Obviously she didn't get the hint last night.

"I am," Bernie says.

I can picture her standing in front of the door, blocking Kimberley's path.

"I'm pretty sure I'm your boss so I suggest you do as you're told and move aside," Kimberley snaps.

That does it. She can be a bitch to me all she likes; I probably deserve it. But Bernie doesn't and I'm not just going to sit here and listen to Kimberley berate her.

"I'm sorry. Would you excuse me for just a moment?" I say to George.

He nods, an amused look on his face. I cross my office with my hands balled into fists at my sides. I can practically feel the steam coming out of my ears. I pull the door open and step outside, pulling it closed behind me.

"Kimberley, what the fuck are you playing at?" I hiss.

"I told you I needed to see you," she says calmly.

Her calm manner only inflates my anger.

"So you thought you'd come here and have a go at Bernie? Who, for the record, is not your subordinate in any way, shape or form."

Bernie beams beside me and moves back to sit behind her desk. She mouths thank you at me and then goes back to her computer, pretending she has no further interest in this exchange. Pretending being the operative word. I can practically see her ears twitching.

"She wouldn't let me in," Kimberley says as though that excuses her shitty behaviour.

I roll my eyes.

"So I heard. As did my client."

"You're really with a client?" she says, looking slightly ashamed of herself.

"Yes," I say. "If I wasn't and I didn't want to see you, I would have just told Bernie to tell you to fuck off."

It's a low blow, telling her I wouldn't even bother having Bernie lie to her to save her feelings, but I'm still pissed about the slanging match Kimberley instigated. It's a good job George seems to have a sense of humour or he could have just walked out.

"Now either sit down, shut up and wait, or leave. It's your call Kimberley."

She looks about ready to blow a fuse, but she can't deny that I'm right to be angry with her and she sits down, biting back her acidic response. I go back into my office.

"I'm so sorry about that George," I say.

"Women trouble?" he smiles.

"Oh you don't know the half of it," I laugh. "I just get all of the aggro and none of the benefits. She's not even my girl. She's just someone I work with."

"She sounds like trouble," George laughs.

"Oh believe me, she is," I say. "Now. Where were we?"

"I was just about to say that I think you're right. I'm definitely swaying towards using your firm. But you mentioned that it wouldn't be you personally handling my business. I wondered if it would be possible to set up a meeting with the person who would be? I like to get a feel for a person before I decide whether or not I want to work with them."

"Of course," I smile. "You'd be working with Bradley, one of our top accountants. Do you want me to see if he's free now or would you prefer to come back?"

"Now works for me," George says.

I call Bradley at his desk and quickly explain the situation.

"Bring him along. I can chat to him now," Bradley says.

I thank him and hang up the call, resisting the urge to punch the air. It's in the bag. Bradley knows his way around this kind of conversation and I think him and George will click. I stand up.

"Follow me and I'll take you to Bradley," I say. "If you're happy to go ahead, he can print out the paperwork and get you all signed up."

"Great," George says, also standing up.

I lead him out of my office. I notice his amused look when he sees Kimberley sitting waiting for me, her head down. I purposely ignore her and focus on Bernie.

"Bernie, could you please see Ms. Montgomery into my office? I'll be back shortly," I say.

"Of course," Bernie beams.

She's already standing up as George and I walk away.

"If you'd like to follow me Ms. Montgomery," Bernie is saying.

Her voice is sweet, fake, dripping with sugar and sarcasm and I grin to myself. If Kimberley is staying here, then she's going to have to learn to get the stick out of her ass when it comes to Bernie.

I lead George to Bradley's desk and introduce them. Bradley is already telling George about his processes when I excuse myself, telling George to let me know if he needs anything else from me.

I head back to my office, a feeling of dread in my stomach. Bernie jumps up when she sees me returning and almost runs around her desk to talk to me.

"God Sebastian, I'm so sorry about that. She just wouldn't take no for an answer," she says.

"That's Kimberley for you," I say. "You don't have to apologise."

"Was the client annoyed?" she asks.

"No, he seemed to find the whole thing quite amusing," I say laughing and shaking my head. "I'd best go and see what her royal highness wants."

Bernie opens her mouth and then closes it again.

"Don't be shy. If you have something to say, spit it out."

"Look I know what she did was unprofessional, but you're in love with her and ..."

"I'm not in love with her," I interrupt.

"Whatever you say," Bernie says, waving away my protest and carrying on where she left off. "And she clearly has feelings for you too. That's why she was acting out. She thought you were alone and just didn't want to see her. Don't be too harsh on her is all I'm saying."

Kimberley was acting out because she's used to clicking her fingers and having me jump to attention. She doesn't like it when she doesn't get her own way. I don't bother trying to explain that to Bernie. She'd only insist I'm still in love with her. Which I'm not.

I nod my head and go to my office door. I take a deep breath and step inside. The door is barely closed when Kimberley jumps to her feet and starts ranting.

"Why didn't you answer my call Sebastian? And what was up with that juvenile text message?" she demands.

Her quiet demeanour from outside of my office is long gone and she's angry now. It makes me even angrier that she gets to burst in here, embarrass me in front of a client and still try to play the victim card.

"Juvenile? Kimberley you burst in here shouting and screaming like a mad woman. You're the one who said you wanted to keep this professional. What part of the stunt you just pulled is professional? The part where you threaten my secretary and accuse her of lying? Or the part where a potential client gets a front row seat to your tantrum?"

Kimberley sighs and raises her hands.

"Guilty as charged. And I'm sorry about that, really I am. I just ... I thought you were avoiding me after the other night."

I roll my eyes.

"We're not teenagers Kimberley. We're adults. Adults fuck and don't spend weeks avoiding each other. I think we can both agree that what happened on Friday was a mistake. We don't need it to be awkward between us because of that. I'm sure we're both perfectly capable of being civil to each other."

"A mistake? Sebastian, it wasn't a mistake. Or at least it wasn't at my end."

"Because perfect Kimberley never makes mistakes," I say.

"I make mistakes. But that wasn't one of them. Sebastian, you were amazing, and I don't regret what happened for a second. We were good together. You know it. I know it. And I'm mature enough to admit that," she says.

I would never admit it to her, but I can admit it to myself. We were good together. The sex was fucking mind blowing. But it wasn't the start of something. It was the end of something,

something that should have been over years ago. Kimberley gets too far under my skin for me to risk going back there.

"Sebastian? Say something for God's sake," Kimberley says. "Just let yourself admit what we did was no mistake."

"Ok. It wasn't a mistake. It was a fun time. But that's all it was. It happening again would be a mistake," I say.

"No. It wouldn't," Kimberley says.

She takes a step towards me. I have to put an end to this conversation right now otherwise I'm not going to be able to stop myself from pulling her into my arms and fucking her right here on my desk. I can't let myself get wrapped up in Kimberley again. I just can't.

"Wow. I guess I was amazing, because you're gagging for it. You remind me of one of those crazy types I occasionally pick up who thinks a one night stand is code for relationship starter. Honestly Kimberley, you're embarrassing yourself coming here begging me for more sex."

Her face falls and I can see tears shining in her eyes.

"You absolute fucking asshole," she hisses, her voice breaking.

She turns and runs from the room. I instantly feel like the most awful person in the world. I can't believe I've made Kimberley cry. I can feel my own heart breaking knowing I've hurt her. I take a step forward. I have to go after her.

I stop. I'll only end up making it worse if I do. And while I never wanted to hurt her, and I know I handled the situation appallingly, I know in my heart I was right. I can't have sex with Kimberley again. I have to distance myself from her so that I can move on.

Kimberley is tough. She'll get over this. Hell she's probably only crying because I embarrassed her. It's not like she's actually into me. She proved that when she walked away from me without so much as a glance back.

A gentle tapping on my office door pulls me out of my head.

"Come in," I say.

Bernie steps in, a concerned look on her face.

"Since when did you start knocking when you know I'm alone?" I say.

She sits down in one of my visitor's chairs.

"She was crying when she left. I thought maybe …"

"You thought maybe I was crying and you didn't want to deal with that hot mess?" I grin.

"I thought maybe you would be upset and want a bit of time to process whatever happened," she corrects me.

I sit down in my own chair and smile at Bernie.

"I'm fine Bernie. Honestly."

She raises an eyebrow, seeing straight through my lie.

"Ok. You got me. I feel bad for making Kimberley cry. That wasn't my intention, but other than a bit of guilt, I'm fine."

"I heard the conversation you two had," Bernie says.

Why doesn't that surprise me?

"I bet you tried really hard not to though huh?" I grin.

"Obviously," she lies with a smile. "Seriously though Sebastian. Why do you keep sabotaging yourself? You're into her.

She's into you. Why not just give it a go? What's the worst thing that could happen?"

She could rip my fucking heart out again for starters I think to myself but don't say.

"Because I can't go there again," I say.

Bernie waits for me to elaborate and I sigh.

"You know when you're with someone and being with them makes you happy, and you become the best version of yourself?" I say.

Bernie nods.

"That's how it used to be with me and Kimberley. But now. Well you've seen it yourself Bernie. Even if I wanted to go there with her again, I can't do it. She brings out the worst in me. Whenever I'm around her, I turn into this petty, bitter shadow of myself. I end up saying or doing something that hurts Kimberley and then I feel bad about it. And I don't like who I am around her. I don't like that guy at all."

"You just have to let go of the old resentments and hurt and let her in," Bernie says.

"That's the thing though Bernie. I can't do that. Believe me, I've tried. This is for the best. We've got closure now and we just need to stay away from each other."

Bernie smiles at me sadly.

"Is that really what you want Sebastian?"

Is it? I think it is. I think it's what I need to do. I do need to let go of the old resentments, but I can't do that with Kimberley hanging around me. I need a clean break from her.

"Yes. I really think it is," I say.

Bernie nods.

"Ok. Then I'll leave you to it. Do you want me to cancel your next meeting?"

I think about it for a second. I'd like nothing more than for Bernie to cancel my meeting. I could just lie on the couch drinking bourbon and thinking about how my life has gone to hell. But I shake my head.

"No thank you," I smile.

I'm not going to waste another minute thinking about Kimberley. And I'm certainly not going to let her affect my work.

I pick up the sandwich and nibble on it. It's good. Chicken salad on rye. The bread is fresh and the salad is nice and crunchy. Matt was right about this place. For a sandwich bar, it's not bad.

"Anything in the works then?" Matt asks me.

"I've always got something in the works," I laugh. "Nothing major though. I know it's been three weeks since we closed the merger, but there's a still a lot of work to do on it to get things running smoothly. I've got an appointment later on today with a new firm though. I'm not sure it'll come to much. They're barely more than a start up and I don't think they'll be able to afford any of our packages, but still. If I make a good impression on them now, who knows what could happen down the line. You?"

"I've got my eye on a new concept restaurant actually," Matt says. "It's one of those fusion places, but they claim to be different to anything already out there. I'm going to talk to them tomorrow. I'm thinking maybe some sort of franchise deal."

"Fusion huh? Like Sushi crossed with curry?"

"It's a bit more sophisticated than that," Matt laughs.

"I like something simple personally. Something where I don't need some sort of degree in food engineering just to work out the menu," I say.

"So you think we should go for low end?" Matt asks raising an eyebrow.

"No. I think we should stick to what works. Classic dishes that people enjoy in a high end setting with good quality ingredients. But hey, what do I know? I'm just talking as a customer here. You're the food guy. Kimberley was always into those fancy places. I'd rather go to a bar and grab a steak."

Matt looks down at his plate but not quickly enough that I don't see him smirking.

"What?" I say. "You can't seriously tell me you don't enjoy a good steak?"

"Who doesn't love steak?" Matt replies. "I'm not laughing at that. I'm laughing at your mention of Kimberley."

"Oh that," I say, rolling my eyes. "Honestly, I'm totally over her Matt. I think I just needed that one last time to really see it. You know, to get closure of whatever. It took a long time, but I can finally see that she's really not that special. I mean she's just a girl right? I haven't even thought of her since she came to my office acting like a brat after we had sex. Until today apparently."

Matt is openly laughing now and I frown.

"What?" I demand. "What the hell is so funny?"

"You trying to claim you haven't thought of Kimberley in weeks. Come on Seb. Who are you trying to kid here? She's all you've talked about since that night."

"What? No she isn't," I insist.

Matt raises an eyebrow.

"We were talking about a restaurant and you managed to bring the conversation around to Kimberley," he says.

"Ok, so I mentioned her once in three weeks. I hardly think that means she's all I talk about."

Do I talk about her a lot? No, surely I don't.

"When we were talking about movies last weekend at mom's place, you talked for like ten minutes about Kimberley's favourite movies. You even managed to turn a conversation about Callie's day working in the library into a conversation about Kimberley's favourite authors the other day."

"I ..." I start.

Matt cuts me off with another laugh.

"I know you're going to try and deny it, but really Seb just give it up. You know Chance's even stopped taking your calls because he's so sick of hearing Kimberley this, Kimberley that."

I open my mouth but I don't have anything to say to that and I close it again. I take a big bite of my sandwich, an excuse not to reply. Matt smiles knowingly at me. Ok, the sandwich trick isn't working. I'll have to meet him half way. I chew the bite and swallow.

"Ok. Maybe I didn't stop thinking about her quite as quickly as I implied. It was a process I suppose. But I'm over her now."

"That's probably a good thing really, you know, considering everything," Matt says.

It's obvious he's holding something back and he's going to make me work to get it out of him. If I refuse to take the bait, he won't be able to resist telling me whatever piece of juicy gossip he has, but still, I take the bait like he knew I would.

"Considering what?" I say.

"Oh just stuff you know."

"For God's sake Matt, just spit it out," I say.

He grins again.

"Well a couple of days ago, Kimberley dropped by my office and she asked me if I thought you would ever come around to her. I thought of all of the times you'd sworn off her and I remembered you saying you were totally over her. So I told her no, I didn't think you would and she should just move on and forget about you."

"Good advice," I say.

I thought I'd be happy to learn Kimberley is the one pining for me, trying to find a way to make me come back to her. I'm not though. I don't like the idea of causing her pain.

"I thought so," Matt says. "Anyway, word is, she has a date. Tonight."

"A date with who?" I demand.

Matt smirks again.

"Why do you care if you're over her?"

"I don't care. I was just making conversation," I say.

"Right," Matt says. "Some guy she met in a club or something. I don't really know."

"Speaking of clubs, how's ours doing?" I ask.

Anything to move the conversation away from Kimberley.

"Good," Matt says. "It's more Chance's area than mine, but he's happy with the profit margins. He's even talking about expanding to a few more so the money must be there."

Some guy she met in a fucking club? He doesn't exactly sound special.

"We should definitely look at that then. Maybe a bar or two as well," I say.

"You just want somewhere you can get a discount when you go out on the sniff," Matt laughs.

"Nothing wrong with that is there?" I say. "How's Callie doing? Did she get that promotion at work?"

Kimberley in a tight dress, some fucking guy with his hands all over her.

"She hasn't heard anything yet. They said it would be next week when she finds out."

"No news is good news right."

I finish up the last of my sandwich. It tastes like cardboard now. The bread suddenly feels too thick and spongey. I swallow down a long swig of water.

"I have to go," I say. "I've got some stuff needs doing."

"Ok," Matt smiles. "It was good to catch up."

"Yeah, sure, whatever," I say.

I have to get away from him before my verbal diarrhoea kicks in and I start talking about Kimberley again. I can't believe she's got a date.

Why do I care? I don't want to date her. She can date whoever the fuck she likes. Fuck her and the space she's still taking up in my head.

~

I check my watch for the hundredth time and see that a whole minute has passed since the last time I checked the time. It's now one minute after seven. It's going to be one whole hell of a long night if I keep checking the time incessantly like this. It's driving me crazy keep checking, but I can't help myself. It's now one minute and seventeen seconds after seven. Kimberley will be getting ready for her date now. But it's ok. I don't care what she's doing or where she's going or who she's going there with. Not even a little bit.

Except I do care. I can't keep lying to myself like this. I do fucking care. I can't stand the thought of Kimberley moving on without me. Not again. Last time, I let her walk out of my life and although it tore me apart, I didn't do a thing to stop her. This time will be different. I might be walking into a bad situation. I might be opening myself up to getting my stupid heart broken yet again, but I don't care. I'm not letting her go without a fight. Not again.

The decision made, I jump up and grab my phone and my keys. I practically sprint from my building and down to my car. I drive straight to Kimberley's hotel and run into the lobby. It's only when I get to the elevators that I realise I have no idea what room number she's staying in. I think for a moment and head to reception.

"Good evening. Can you tell me where I might find a Ms Kimberley Montgomery please?" I say.

"I'm sorry sir," the receptionist replies. "I'm not allowed to give out that information."

I could play the star crossed lovers card. Tell her that I'm here to win back the girl who broke my heart four years ago and beg her to understand. But that might not work. I know what will though. I give the woman my most charming smile.

"I understand that, but this is an emergency. I work with Kimberley and she has exactly twenty minutes to fix a major mistake or she'll be fired. I'm giving her a chance here, a head's up before her boss catches on. I can't call her. Company phone. If they investigate the mistake, which believe me they will when they see it's cost them billions, then I don't want a call to be on the record. So I guess it's your call. Follow the rules and get Kimberley fired, or take a walk back there and let me take a peek at the guest book."

"I ... ummmm," she starts.

"Come on. Put yourself in her shoes. If you were her, wouldn't you rather someone told me your room number rather than let you get fired and lose your whole career?"

She is starting to come around and I smile again. I have one more trick up my sleeve. One I know will push her decision for her. I'm not going to put her in the same imaginary boat as the one I've put Kimberley in. Surely she'll want to save her own skin.

"Just between me and you, her father owns this hotel chain. If he was to find out that his own staff could have saved his daughter's career, and chose not to help ..."

"I'm sorry. I can't help you," she says loudly. She winks at me then looks pointedly down at a spot beside her computer where the guest register sits. "Now if you'll excuse me, I have work to do."

She turns and walks through a door behind reception, her heels clacking as she walks. She's let me know where to find the information but done it in a way that can't come back to bite her on the ass. She clearly told me she couldn't help me and then took herself out of the situation before it could escalate. Something I know for a fact large hotel chains train their staff to do. If they ever watch this CCTV footage, which I'm sure they won't, they won't see her wink at me or direct my gaze to the register. She'll be in the clear. Besides, even if Kimberley refuses to talk to me, she'll blame me entirely for this. She won't try and get the receptionist fired. It's not her style. She knows I can be very persuasive when I want to be.

I pull the register towards me and scan down the guest list looking for her name. It jumps out at me like it's lit up in neon. Kimberley Montgomery. Room five ninety three. I go back to the elevator and slip inside. I go up to the fifth floor and follow the directions on the wall until I'm at Kimberley's room.

I pause for a moment. This is my last chance to back out. I could just turn around and leave and put Kimberley behind me. That would be the sensible thing to do. But I've played it safe too long and look where it's gotten me. A bunch of empty one night stands.

I reach up and knock on the door. It is opened quickly and I find Kimberley staring out at me.

She's wearing a short black dress, black sky scraper peep toe shoes and her hair is softly curled and hangs around her face. Damn. She looks amazing. Her date wouldn't have been able to keep his dirty fucking hands off her. It's a good job I'm here to make sure she never gets anywhere near him.

"You look beautiful," I say before I can stop myself.

She smiles but then she catches herself and raises an eyebrow.

"What are you doing here Sebastian?" she asks with a sigh.

"I came to borrow a cup of sugar," I grin.

She rolls her eyes but she steps back from the door. I go inside and close it before she can change her mind. It isn't so much a room she's staying in as a suite. I am standing in what looks like a high end lounge complete with a large, plush looking white couch with a wooden trim and a huge TV opposite it. A low coffee table has been pushed to one side. Doors open off the room which I assume lead to the bedrooms and the bathroom. A large glass door leads to a balcony which is big enough for three sun loungers, a table and four chairs.

"Nice room," I say. "It's almost as big as my apartment."

"Yes. And it has the advantage of room service and a cleaner. You didn't come here to talk me about my hotel room though did you? I don't have all day. I'm on my way out. Now what do you want?" she says.

"Where are you going?" I ask, stalling because I'm suddenly not sure I'm ready for the grand gesture anymore.

"None of your damned business," she retorts.

I move closer to her, inching in until I'm standing close enough to her that our bodies are almost touching. I lean my head even closer until I can feel her hair tickling my skin. I tuck it behind her ear. She doesn't stop me. I whisper into her ear.

"Wherever it is, you're sure going to make an impression. You're stunning."

She looks down and smiles up at me through her long eyelashes. My cock is twitching, hardening, ready for her. I reach out and gently stroke her face.

"That dress looks great on you," I say.

She steps back, laughing and shaking her head. Well shit. I actually thought my charm was working on her. I should have known better. Kimberley isn't one for compliments. She prefers real talk. She always has. If I want to get her to stay, I'll have to come up with something of substance. Something that will make it worth her while to stick around for.

"You're going to have to do better than that if you want to get back into my good books Sebastian," she says. "Now if you don't mind, like I said, I'm on my way out."

She picks up her handbag and moves towards the door. I remind myself that I'm not going to let her walk away from me again. It's time for the grand gesture whether I'm ready or not.

"I missed you too," I blurt out.

She looks back at me and for a second her face softens, but then it hardens again and she shakes her head.

"Too little too late Sebastian," she says softly.

She wants to believe me though. She wants to stay. If she didn't, she would be out of the door now. I just have to find a way to let her stay without losing face.

"I tell you what, I'll do you a deal," I say. "Rock paper scissors. If I win, you stay and we talk. If you win, I'll leave."

"What are you talking about? Why do you even want me to stay after you were so adamant that what happened between us was a mistake?" she says.

"I was stupid to say that. Now stop avoiding the question. Are we playing?" I ask.

I smile at her and watch as she softens again. She never could stay mad at me for long. I know I've almost convinced her. She glances at the door and then back at me. I could still lose her. She could still tell me to take a hike. I have to push it slightly, make her stay.

"What's the matter Kimberley? Are you scared you'll lose?"

"No. I just can't work out what's in it for me. Why would I stay?"

"Because you get the pleasure of my company all evening," I smile. "And if you win, then you can go out and enjoy your night on a high."

She shakes her head but she's laughing.

"Fine. You're on," she says.

She comes back towards me and stands a couple of feet away.

"On three?" she asks.

I nod and we count together.

"One. Two. Three."

We draw and Kimberley goes for rock just like I knew she would. It means she wants to stay. It was a running joke between us when we were younger that Kimberley always went for rock at this game. She must remember that. She knows I do and she knows I'll go for paper and beat her. If she didn't want to stay, she wouldn't have gone for rock. I go for paper, just Kimberley knew I would, and I smirk at her.

"Looks like you got all dressed up for nothing," I say.

She looks ready to argue with me, even now knowing I know she chose to stay, she is still so scared of losing face that she's acting like she's kind of pissed off to have lost the game, but she puts her handbag down beside her as she sits down on the couch.

A game is a game and while Kimberley doesn't lose games often, when she does, she'll pout like hell but she'll suffer the consequences. Although I'd like to think an evening in my company is more pleasurable than suffering.

"Well? You wanted to talk and now you've got me here. So talk," she says.

She pulls her phone out and begins to type out a text. I sit down beside her and try to take her phone away from her.

"No pouting. You knew the rules of the game," I say.

She keeps her grip on her phone.

"I'm not pouting. I'm cancelling my plans," she says. "I agreed to stay but I didn't agree to be rude about it."

She makes a fair point and I nod and gesture at her to carry on. She finishes sending the text and puts her phone away. That's a good sign.

"You wanted to talk, yet still you're not. Are you still playing a game Seb? Did you just want to prove to yourself that you still have power over me? Or do you actually want to discuss things? I can't fathom you out. Now tell me one thing and be honest. Why now?"

"Four years ago, you walked out of my life and broke my heart," I say.

"Oh not this again," she says.

She goes to stand up and I put my hand on her knee and shake my head. She relaxes back into the couch. She looks at my hand but she doesn't push it away and I leave it there when I continue talking.

"Just hear me out ok? It's not an accusation, I promise. You walked out of my life and broke my heart. I've held that against you every day since you left. It's taken me this long to realise something. You walked away from me because I let you go. Well this time, I'm not going to make the same mistake. I'm not just going to let you walk out of my life again Kimberley."

She looks into my eyes as she answers me.

"I didn't want to walk away this time Sebastian. You pushed me away remember."

Her eyes haven't left mine. They flit side to side slightly like she's trying to read the answers directly from my brain.

"I'm not pushing you away now am I?" I say.

I can almost see the sparks flying between us as I hold her gaze with mine, willing her to forgive me. There's so much I want to say, so much I want to fix between us, but I don't even know where to start. I haven't got the words to tell her everything I want her to know. I just have to hope she can see it all in my eyes.

Maybe she does because before I really know what's happening, her hands are on my shoulders and she's pushing me back against the couch. She hooks her leg over mine and straddles me. I push my hands into her hair and pull her face towards mine, bringing my lips up to meet hers.

We kiss like we've been unleashed. Our hands are all over each other, exploring, caressing, probing. Kimberley's tongue is my mouth; her scent is in my nose. She is consuming me once more. I kiss her like my life depends on it. Maybe it does. Maybe it always did.

My cock is hard, straining to be free of my jeans as Kimberley moves her hips, grinding against it. She unbuttons my shirt and pushes it down my arms, throwing it to one side. I grab the hem of her dress and pull it over her head, throwing it down with my shirt. I pull her mouth back to mine as I unhook her bra.

She runs her nails over my bare chest, sending shivers through me as I hungrily kiss her. I reach up and caress her breasts, feeling her hard nipples against my palms. She sucks in a sharp breath as I pinch her nipples in my fingers and roll them, making them even harder. She throws her head back and I run my tongue down her neck, over her chest. I suck one of her breasts into my mouth and work my tongue over her nipple.

"I need you to fuck me Sebastian. Now," she says breathily.

"Yes ma'am," I eagerly agree.

I lift my hips up, moving Kimberley back slightly. I fumble my belt open with one hand, my other hand on Kimberley's back, and then I open my jeans. I hold Kimberley in place with one hand as I lift my ass up from the couch. I pull my jeans and boxers down with one hand. I sit back down and kiss Kimberley again. I take the sides of her panties in my hands and tear them off her.

She gasps as I throw her torn underwear to one side. She grins down at me, her lips swollen and red from all of the kissing. Her eyes are filled with lust as she looks at me.

I grab my cock as she lifts herself slightly and positions herself over it. I can feel the heat coming off her pussy and as I put my cock against her opening, I feel how wet she is. I moan as I enter her, stretching her pussy, claiming her as mine once more.

I push inside of her sweet folds, and she grips me, her pussy tight around me. She begins to move up and down on my cock and I can feel my pulse racing, my breathing speeding up as she moves faster.

I push my hands into her hair again and bring her face down to mine. She resists me for a moment, rubbing her lips lightly over mine, teasing me and making me want her more. I push harder on her head and she stops teasing me, her mouth clamping onto mine, her tongue massaging mine. I run my hands up and down her back, enjoying the feel of her naked skin that's damp with sweat.

She nibbles on my lower lip as I slam my cock into her over and over again, pushing her towards the edge. Her breathing quickens as she moves with me, matching my thrusts with fevered thrusts of her own. Her breasts are moving in time with her thrusting. She pulls back from me, throwing her head back, her face contorted as she moans.

I can see the pulse in her neck as the tendons stand out as her orgasm floods her. I feel her pussy clenching around my cock, driving me wild, bringing me closer to my own climax. It's all I can do to hold myself back but I want to watch Kimberley. She is a Goddess, a vision of beauty as she rides my cock, screaming out her pleasure as I slam off her g-spot. A warm rush of liquid floods out of her, drenching me in her juices.

I plunge into her again and she screams my name. She puts her hands on my shoulders, using them to push herself up and down even faster. Her nails dig into my shoulders as she comes again. I feel another clench, another flood of liquid and I can't hold back any longer. I come hard, feeling my orgasm in every pore of my body.

"Oh my God, Kimberley," I shout as I spurt into her.

My cock is going wild, sending waves of pleasure through my body, the tingling feeling taking my breath away for a moment. I am rigid, coming hard. I suck in a breath as the feeling starts to fade, leaving behind a warm, sated feeling. Kimberley collapses forward against my chest and I hold her in my arms, stroking her hair and whispering her name as we both fight to get our breaths back.

Finally, she looks up at me with a lazy smile.

"So that was a good opening line. Did you have anything else you wanted to say?" she asks, her tone flirty, her eyes telling me she wants more.

"Oh believe me, there's a whole lot more where that came from," I tell her.

"Right answer," she smiles.

She gets up off my lap, and stands up, I look her up and down, taking in every inch of her naked body. Just looking at her like this, her skin shiny and glowing, has my cock standing at attention once more. Her eyes go to my cock and she smiles again, greedily this time. I follow her gaze, noting the slick layer of her juices coating my cock and my upper thighs.

Kimberley doesn't say anything else, she just falls to her knees before me. I swallow hard as she reaches out and takes my cock in her fist. She blows lightly on the end of it as her hand begins to stroke my length. Her warm breath sends shock waves through my body and I close my eyes, resting my head back against the back of the couch. They fly open again when Kimberley plunges her mouth over me, taking my full length into her mouth and throat.

"Holy shit," I whisper as her head begins to bob up and down, her rough little tongue flicking over my cock and sending me straight back to the edge.

My hands ball into fists beside me as Kimberley works me. She sucks hard and fast, just the way I like it, bringing me to the edge in seconds. One of her hands works the base of my cock and the other kneads my ball sack. I reach down and stop her, moving her head away from me. As much as I never want her to stop sucking me, I have to stop her. I don't want to come in her mouth. I want to come in her pussy.

She seems to understand and she gets to her feet again. She smiles down at me and takes her nipples between her fingers. She puts her head back, her eyes closed as she touches herself. Her nipples are hard in her grasp as she rolls them back and forth between her fingers.

I reach out to rub my fingers through her slit but she must have her eyes open a touch because she steps back out of my reach, shaking her head. She's teasing me again, putting on a show, but it's the kind of show I could watch all night long.

One of her hands leaves her nipple and moves down her stomach to her pussy. She pushes her fingers between her lips and begins to play with herself. I am tempted to grab my cock and jerk off as I watch her, but I want to save myself for when I am inside of her again.

I sit back and watch the show. It's hard to enjoy it when there's this insistent voice in my head telling me to grab Kimberley and fuck her again, but I realise I don't want to fuck her. I want to make love to her.

"Kimberley," I say, my voice full of lust for her.

She opens her eyes and looks at me, but she doesn't stop playing with herself. She's panting now and the sound is so distracting, the look on her face pulling me back into her show. The words die on my lips and I just sit there, watching her.

She brings herself to the edge, sending herself tumbling through another orgasm. She looks me straight in the eye as she comes hard, moaning my name, and then she pulls her fingers away from herself. She moves into my reach again and I wrap my arms around her waist, shuffling to the edge of the couch so that I can feel her body against mine. She pushes the fingers she used on her clit into my mouth and I can taste her juices, like salt and sugar. I lick her fingers, eagerly cleaning her juices off, savouring the taste of them, of her.

She pulls her fingers back out of my mouth and backs away from me again. She beckons to me and I stand up and go to her.

"The bedroom," she whispers.

I think she feels the same as I do. That this time, we'll be making love, slower, more tender. I let her take my hand and lead me across the lounge. I hold my open jeans and boxers up with the other hand as I follow her. I would follow her anywhere right now in any state of undress. She opens a door and leads me into a small hallway. She points to the door on our left.

"In there," she says.

I step into her bedroom. She follows close behind me. I don't waste any time. I move to the side of the bed and kick my trainers and socks off. I push my jeans and boxer shorts the rest of the way down and get onto the bed. Kimberley climbs on beside me and we lay for a moment, on our sides, looking into each other's eyes.

Kimberley's eyes are hard to read. I want to ask her what she's thinking, but I'm suddenly afraid of the answer. If she starts throwing the L word around, I'm afraid I'll panic and say something stupid. Instead of speaking and risking destroying the moment, I lean closer and kiss her again. Our kiss is slow and sensual, the frenzied desperation from before spent, replaced with a sated feeling that tells me we're going to spend a long time exploring each other, kissing each other, connecting with each other.

Kimberley runs her fingernails up and down my back gently as we kiss. I put my hand on her hip, caressing her with my thumb. I push her onto her back and kiss down her neck and chest. I run my tongue along her stomach, moving lower. I watch as her skin puckers slightly at my touch. I skip her pussy, although I want nothing more to dive right back in there.

I scoot down the bed and pick up one of Kimberley's feet. I run my fingers over her ankles and up her calf. I take her other foot and massage it lightly and then I run my fingers over that calf and over her knee. I crawl back up slightly and run my hands up her inner thighs. She moans as I lightly touch her, bringing goose bumps to the surface of her skin.

I lean forward and kiss her belly and then her pubic bone, before I finally allow myself to plunge my tongue inside of her warm lips. She's still so wet, so ready for this. I can taste the need in her juices as I run my tongue over her clit. She gasps as I work her. I lick her slowly, bringing her body to life with long, almost lazy strokes of my tongue. I want to make her wait, make her experience the build up to her climax before she's plunged right into it. I want her to be desperate for it when it hits her.

I lick through her slit, moving back to her pussy. I push my tongue inside of her, feeling her tight little pussy clenching around it. I move it in and out of her, and she gasps again. I run my hands down the sides of her body, bringing her skin to life again as I continue to tongue fuck her. I move my tongue back through her slit to her clit, flicking my tongue over it lightly.

She makes a whimpering sound.

"Sebastian please," she whispers.

She starts to move her hips, thrusting her clit against my tongue. I ignore her desperate pleas and reach down from her sides and pin her hips to the bed, holding her still as I continue to tease her clit slowly.

Her pleas become more fevered, she's practically begging me to give her some release. I smile to myself and up the pace of my licking. I feel her rigid muscles relax as I bring her to the edge. I suck her clit into my mouth, running my tongue over it and pressing it against the roof of my mouth. She moans, a long, low sound, that becomes a scream as I suck harder, finally bringing her over the edge.

I can feel her clit pulsing as I hold it in my mouth. I release her hips and they lift from the mattress as she gasps for breath as her whole body comes to life. I release her clit and move my lips back up her body as she comes hard.

I find her mouth with mine and push my tongue into her mouth. She puts her hands into my hair, tugging it into her fists as her orgasm seizes her. She moans loudly into my mouth and then she gasps in a breath. She moves her head, nuzzling her face against my neck as she pants for air. Her breath sends shivers through me as it tickles my skin.

She wraps her arms around my shoulders, holding herself tightly against me as her body arches, and then finally, she's still again. She puts her head back onto the pillow and looks at me, her eye lids heavy.

"Shit Sebastian, that was ... something else," she breathes.

I kiss her, stopping her from saying anything else, anything that could ruin the moment between us, and she kisses me back, still holding me against her. I can feel her nipples pressing against my chest and I can feel the heat coming off her pussy, making my cock respond to her call.

I reach down and line my cock up with her pussy and then I push myself inside of her again. She sucks in a breath as I fill her up and she pulls back from me, looking into my eyes, biting her bottom lip.

"Make love to me Sebastian," she says in an almost shy voice. It's not like her usual demanding tone that she uses when she wants something. It's softer; a request rather than an order. One I am happy to fulfil.

I move slowly inside of Kimberley, long, sensual strokes that tease us both, awakening every nerve in both of our bodies. Kimberley wraps her legs around my waist, pushing me in deeper as we move as one. She is wet and slippery and tight and it takes everything I have not to move faster, not to pound into her. I want to make her feel loved, special.

I can feel her pussy starting to clench around me and her body is shaking beneath me as her orgasm washes over her. The slow build up does nothing to spoil the intensity of Kimberley's orgasm. It floods through her full body, turning her to jelly beneath me as she whispers my name over and over.

I come up onto my knees, holding Kimberley against me. She flops against my chest, her head resting on my shoulder as she experiences a deep rooted pleasure that holds her full body under its spell. I hold her hips, moving her up and down on me until finally my own release comes. It's so intense I can't breathe for a moment as it slams through my body, sending me into a wall of ecstasy. I hold Kimberley tightly against me as I fight to breathe, to move.

I relax and let my orgasm take me. I can feel my cock twitching wildly, fire exploding through my stomach and out into every part of my body. I can feel Kimberley still shaking in my arms as her orgasm starts to fade. I thrust into her again, hard, as I spurt once more and she screams out loud as another orgasm slams through her body. We clutch each other as we both tumble through waves of fire until finally, I feel my senses start to return to me and my muscles turn to warm, satisfied jelly.

Kimberley lifts her head from my shoulder with an effort and pushes her lips against mine. I kiss her gently, whispering her name into her mouth. She just clings to me, kissing me, barely in control of herself.

I hold her to me and lay down on my side. She shuffles closer, pressing herself against me as I wrap my arm around her waist. I am so tired after what we've just done, but I don't want to miss a moment with Kimberley and I force my eyes to stay open so I can watch her fall asleep. Her eyes gently close and I watch her face relax, her lips part slightly. Her grip on me doesn't relax and we lay holding each other tightly for a long time before I lose my fight and sleep finally takes me.

Chapter Fourteen

KIMBERLEY

I wake up and glance at the clock. It's only just after four and I wonder what woke me. I am usually a pretty heavy sleeper. Memories of last night start to come back in when I move slightly and feel the dull ache between my legs. Sebastian came here and made me feel things I didn't know I could feel. I realise I can still feel his presence and that's what must have woke me. I turn over looking for him, but he's not laid beside me. He's sitting on the end of the bed, looking out at the city. I shuffle down the bed and wrap my arms around him from behind. I kiss his neck, smelling his scent and feeling my pussy respond to him.

"Are you ok?" I ask.

He reaches up and rubs his hand over mine.

"Yeah. I'm fine. Just thinking," he says.

I kiss his shoulder and then move to sit beside him.

"Why did you come here tonight Sebastian? Why now? And don't give me any shit about a cup of sugar," I say with a soft laugh.

He turns to look at me and gives me the smile that melts me inside.

"You really want to know?" he asks.

I nod my head. I need to know. I need to know if this is anything real or if it's just Sebastian being Sebastian again. I need to know if he's going to shut me out again like he did last time we had sex.

"I found out you had a date tonight. And although I tried to tell myself I didn't care, obviously I did care. I cared enough to come here and try to stop you from seeing someone else."

"So you're officially my stalker now," I laugh. "Good to know."

He laughs with me.

"Yeah. Something like that," he agrees.

"Well if you're going to keep doing it, I suggest you find better intel," I smile. "I wasn't going on a date. I was meeting some old friends for drinks. Female friends."

Sebastian frowns for a second and then he laughs. His laughter is infectious and I find myself joining in with it.

"It proves one thing though," I say.

"Oh? And what's that?"

"You don't hate me half as much as you claim to," I say. "In fact, I'd go as far as to say you don't hate me at all."

Sebastian shakes his head.

"I've never hated you Kimberley," he says, looking deep into my eyes.

The moonlight streaming in through the window makes his eyes look even more intense and I feel my clit throbbing from the way he looks at me. He laughs and the moment is gone.

"Although in the beginning, I really fucking tried to."

I bump my shoulder against his and for the first time, I feel like we're no longer running away from each other or pushing each other away. I scoot backwards on the bed and get back under the covers as the chilly night air begins to take effect on me. I pat the bed beside me and Sebastian scoots up too. We lay down facing each other.

"I'm so sorry for hurting you Sebastian all those years ago. It was never my intention," I say.

He shrugs with one shoulder.

"It's in the past now isn't it?"

"It is. But I feel like we need to get it all out. To say everything we wished we could have said back then."

"Ok. You want honest so I'll give you honest," Sebastian says. "Like I said earlier, I've blamed you for a long time for what happened between us, but the truth is, I let you walk away without fighting for you. But I still don't understand why you left at all."

"I wanted a career. Is that really so hard for you to understand? Even after all of these years?"

"Of course not. I wanted a career myself. But what's still hard for me to understand is why you thought we couldn't have both. You knew my dad would have given you a job, mentored you. Why did you have to leave me to have a career?"

I pause for a moment and shake my head.

"Because I needed to prove to myself that I could do this alone. I needed to know that I could have a career based on what I could do rather than who I knew. I love your dad Seb, you know that. But taking a job from him, no matter how good at it I was, there would have always been doubts in the back of my mind. I would have always wondered if I was really good at my job, or if I was there because I was your girlfriend and your dad felt like he couldn't get rid of me."

Sebastian smiles.

"You're really overestimating my dad's character. If you were rubbish, you'd have been gone whether I liked it or not. He would sack me or my brothers if we let him down."

"I can see that now. But I couldn't back then," I admit. "I was so young when I left, and yet I had no problem moving away from home. Leaving this city, my family, none of it fazed me. But leaving you? That was the hardest thing I ever did."

"Why didn't you tell me all of this at the time Kimberley instead of just ending things between us? I'd have come with you. Hell I would have followed you anywhere back then."

"And that's why I couldn't ask you to come with me. I know you would have done it. And even though you were hesitant about working for your dad, I knew deep down it's what you wanted. I didn't want to be the reason you walked away from the family business. You want to know the really ironic thing?"

Sebastian nods.

"I didn't want you to come with me and wake up one morning a year, two years, down the line and realise you made a terrible mistake." I laugh softly. "I didn't want you to resent me."

"Well you sure fucked that up," Sebastian says with a laugh.

I laugh with him even though my heart is breaking a little. Because he's right. I did fuck up. I fucked up big time.

"Didn't I just," I say.

I reach up and stroke his face.

"I would never leave you again," I say.

Sebastian places his hand over mine and gently moves it from his face.

"Don't make promises you can't keep Kimberley," he says.

"No, you don't understand," I say.

"I do understand," he replies. "And I'm not trying to be a dick. You can't say for sure your career won't take you somewhere else is all I mean. But we're older now. Some might say wiser. And we could make it work if it's what we both want. Without you having to compromise your career."

I feel tears fill my eyes and I blink them away quickly.

"Are you saying you're willing to try?" I ask.

He nods.

"Yeah. But there have to be some boundaries. As easy as it would be to fall back into our old patterns, we work together now, and I think we can both agree that we've put far too much of ourselves into this merger to throw it all away because we realise we're not the same people we used to be and things won't work between us."

I open my mouth to protest, but Sebastian puts his finger on my lips. His touch sends shivers through me and I fall silent.

"I'm not saying it won't work Kimberley. I'm saying we don't know how it's going to go. And that's ok. But we need to be sure before we make any sort of promises to each other."

"So what are you saying Sebastian?" I ask.

"I'm saying I'm willing to try if you are. But that we should take things slow, keep it casual for now and see how it goes. And we both need to learn to separate business from pleasure."

I feel myself nodding.

"Yeah. That makes sense," I say.

"You sound disappointed," Sebastian says.

"I'm not," I lie.

"Yes. You are," he says. "If this stands any chance of working, then we have to be honest with each other. I know you were hoping for more. Some grand gesture where I sweep you off your feet and we run off into the sunset together. But I'm just not ready for that Kimberley. Once bitten and twice shy and all that."

"Ok," I say, nodding. "I get it. But if we're being honest, then I need to say something. If we have any chance of making it work, you have to find a way to forgive me for leaving you. Because if you can't do that, then that will always be hanging over us."

"I know. I can't promise I can do that yet though. Which is why I said we need to take things slowly. I can promise I will try though. Is that enough for you Kimberley? Because if it isn't, then say now."

I think about it for a moment. Is it enough? I really hope so because although the merger was a good business move, for me, that was never really what this was about. I came back here for Sebastian. There I said it. Can I do this knowing he might never forgive me?

If I want him back, then I guess I'll have to. I can't wave a magic wand and make him forgive me. But I can show him that I'm serious about us. I can show him that every day until he sees it for himself and then surely he'll forgive me.

I feel myself nodding and I start to smile. Of course it's enough. It's better than anything I could have expected. Even Matt told me I was wasting my time. That Sebastian would never come around and I should just move on. But here he is willing to try.

"Yes," I say. "It's enough that you're here with me and you're willing to try."

He leans closer and kisses me and any remaining doubts I have float away. His words tell me he's not ready to forgive me, but his kiss tells me something else entirely. His kiss tells me he'll never ever let me go again.

I move closer to him, pulling his body against mine. I need to feel every part of him touching every part of me so I can convince myself this is real. I can feel his hard cock pressing against me, and what started out as a tender kiss soon becomes deeper, more passionate. I can feel my body responding to Sebastian as his hands roam over my bare skin. My clit throbs and although it feels tender and sore, I don't care. I need to have Sebastian. Now.

I push him onto his back and roll with him, still kissing him. I lay on top of him, my tongue probing into his mouth. His hands move up and down my back, onto my ass. He is breathing heavier now, and I know he's as ready for this as I am. I push myself up so I am straddling him. I move my hips, rubbing my dripping wet pussy over his cock and he gasps. I grin down at him and then I reach behind myself and take his cock in my fist. I work him, listening to the way his breathing hitches.

When he moans my name, I feel my pussy clench, produced a rush of warm liquid and I have to have him inside of me right now. I lift my hips and run the tip of his cock through my lips, letting him feel just how wet for him I am. He moans again and I line him up with my pussy and push myself back down, taking him inside of me. I wince slightly as my already raw pussy stretches to accommodate his huge cock.

I begin to move up and down, slowly at first, teasing him. He brings his hand down and works my clit with his fingers as I move. His touch makes me wince as my sensitive clit throbs. The pain of having him touch me again so soon recedes quickly, leaving behind a fiery feeling of such intense pleasure I feel myself throwing my head back.

My hips start to move quicker of their own accord as I feel my climax building. I can feel Sebastian's cock rubbing against my g-spot and his fingers work me effortlessly, sending my body into over drive.

"Oh my God, Sebastian, don't stop," I shout as he thrusts his hips with mine, making each stroke deeper.

My orgasm hits me like a blinding wave that's so intense that for a moment I can't breathe, can't think. It fires through my whole body, sending me wild, setting nerves firing every-where. I freeze, paralysed for a moment as Sebastian continues to thrust, his probing fingers making my clit sing. The release floods me, warm waves of pleasure cascading through my body, my pussy clenching and flooding. Sebastian moans as my pussy tightens around him and then he's coming too, his warm seed filling me, uniting us in our mutual pleasure.

I come back to myself as Sebastian's cock slips out of me and I move to lay beside him. I rest my head on his chest, feeling it moving up and down. I move my fingers over his chest and stomach, loving the taut muscular feel to it.

"Is that slow enough for you?" I whisper when I've got my breath back.

He gives a soft laugh and squeezes my hand. I'm starting to fall back to sleep when I feel Sebastian shift. I open my eyes and look up at him. He smiles at me and kisses the tip of my nose.

"I should go," he says.

I nod my head, reminding myself we're taking it slow. I don't want him to go, but I don't want to look like some desperate woman who can't let Sebastian out of my sight for two minutes. That's not the way to get him back. The way to get him back is just by being myself, and if it wasn't for our history, I'd want him to go. I'd want to leave him wanting more.

I shuffle back so my head is on the pillow and smile at Sebastian,

"I guess I'll see you at the office in a couple of hours," I say.

Chapter Fifteen

SEBASTIAN

It's been two weeks since Kimberley and I talked. We're still taking things slowly, but it's going well so far. We've seen each other a few times each week and it's been nice. Like old times but different. We've both changed a lot, but I think the changes have all been for the better. We've grown up a bit, got more worldly, but ultimately, we're the same people and we still have that same connection we had all of those years ago. We just communicate a lot more openly now.

For now, we've agreed to keep our arrangement between just us until we're both sure this is what we really want. It's going to be hard to keep up the charade today at my parents' house, but it's a Sunday tradition that we all spend the day together as a family and Kimberley and I have both been busy with work and haven't managed to see each other since Thursday. We've texted and called each other but it's not the same. So I have invited Kimberley to come to the house and spend the day with us. It won't seem that unusual; Kimberley knows my whole family well and my mum has never objected to us bringing friends along before. She'll be happy to see Kimberley, I know that much, I'm just worried she'll read too much into it and create a lot of pressure for us.

I park my car up and head up to the house. Within seconds of stepping in, I know inviting Kimberley to join us was a mistake. My mum greets me with a knowing smile and Matt and Callie both give me big cheesy grins and thumbs ups as I take a seat in the lounge. Only my dad seems oblivious to what's going on. He glances up from his paper and greets me and then goes back to reading.

"What?" I say to Matt and Callie after I say hi to my dad.

"Nothing," Callie giggles.

"We're just pleased to see you," Matt puts in. "Is that a crime now?"

"Stop it," mum chastises them. She turns her focus onto Matt. "You didn't get this abuse when you brought Callie here did you?"

"No," Matt says. "But I didn't try to pretend we were just friend's did I?"

"And I'm not pretending," I insist. "It is possible for two people of the opposite sex to be friends you know. I mean I've brought Bernie here before and there was no fanfare."

"I'm not saying it's not possible for you to be just friends with a woman Seb. I'm saying it's not possible for you to be just friends with Kimberley," Matt teases me.

The doorbell goes and mum hurries off to answer it.

"Stop it now. Both of you," I hiss when I hear my mum greeting Kimberley.

"Hi Kimberley," Matt says, standing up to hug her. "I can't believe Seb didn't pick you up."

Kimberley raises an eyebrow.

"And there was me thinking it's not the 1900s and I'm perfectly capable of driving myself somewhere. How silly of me."

Matt laughs and Kimberley grins at him. She can handle his taunting so much better than I ever could. Matt introduces her to Callie. Callie hugs her and Kimberley sits down beside her. They chat away like they've known each other for years. I was a little worried Callie would be cold to her after she said she doesn't sound like a nice person, but obviously Matt has convinced her I'm the asshole rather than Kimberley.

I can't help but watch Kimberley as she chats. My eyes are drawn to her and I'm hyper aware of every little move she makes, every time she laughs. I catch myself staring and look away quickly, but not before Matt and mum have noticed.

I am saved from any further embarrassment for now when Chance comes in.

"About time," dad says to him, finally putting his paper down now everyone has arrived.

"Hey it's not like I was out socialising dad," Chance says. "I've been in the office working on a new design."

"No work talk," mum cautions him.

He holds his hands up and laughs.

"Right, well then call dad off," he says.

"Carlton," mum says in a warning voice. "You work him too hard. How will he ever meet a nice girl if he's tied to the office all day every day?"

"Well Sebastian managed it," Matt says.

The heat didn't stay off me for long. I glare at him and he laughs.

"Right. Enough. Dinner before you all end up killing each other," mum laughs.

We go through to the dining room and mum brings the food through. There's enough for double the amount of people as always. Kimberley is talking to my dad, telling him about how she managed to land her job. I notice mum doesn't tell her off for talking about work, but I don't comment on it.

"Is this the first time you've met Kimberley?" mum asks Callie.

She nods her head.

"Ah she's like one of the family. Growing up, her and Sebastian were inseparable. They practically lived at each other's houses."

"Ok, enough," I say.

Mum ignores me and carries on.

"We were planning on going away one Christmas. Kimberley's parents wouldn't let her come because they said Christmas was for family. Sebastian refused to eat for days until eventually, we just gave up on the idea and didn't go away."

"Mum, really. No one cares," I say, feeling myself blushing. "We were just kids then."

"But now you're both all grown up and you've found your way back to each other. Just like I always knew you would."

Everyone is listening to mum reminiscing now and I feel myself blushing more.

"Do you think we could talk about something else? Like literally anything else?" I say. "Isn't it about time you started bothering Callie to make you a grandma or something?"

It's Callie's turn to blush and Matt glares at me. I give him an innocent smile. My mum smiles at my dad.

"That's why Carlton built us this house. He said it was too big when I told him about the home I dreamed of, but I insisted it wasn't. I wanted it to be big enough so that when you three grew up and had kids of your own, there was always enough room for everyone to stay over. I wanted the house to be full of love and laughter and children."

"I think you might be waiting a while before that happens," Matt laughs. "Callie and I are happy as we are for now, Chance is married to the job. And well, Sebastian is single."

He puts single in air quotes which I choose to ignore. Kimberley tenses up beside me but it's only for a second and then she relaxes again and I think maybe I imagined it.

"Would you excuse me for a second?" Kimberley says, standing up.

I didn't imagine it. I glare at Matt as Kimberley leaves the room.

"Nice," I say.

"Oh come on Seb. She can't be upset because I said you were single when the two of you are both pretending you're not back together."

I keep glaring at him and he shakes his head.

"Let me go talk to her," he says.

"No. I'll go," I say.

I get up and head out after Kimberley. I find her coming back towards the dining room.

"Are you alright?" I ask.

"I'm fine," she smiles. "I just needed to use the bathroom. Any reason you felt the need to follow me?"

"I ... I thought you were upset because Matt said I was single," I admit.

Kimberley laughs.

"Matt doesn't think you're single. He just wants to hear you admit it," she says. "And no, I'm not upset by his comments. Seriously Sebastian, you have to stop letting him get under your skin the way he does. That's why he winds you up."

I smile and shake my head.

"Yeah. You're right. Come on, we'd better get back before they plan our whole wedding and name our first born," I say.

Kimberley laughs and follows me back to the dining room. We retake our seats. The atmosphere in the room has changed. No one seems to quite know what to say. Kimberley kicks me under the table and gives me a pointed look. I know what she wants. She wants me to make a joke and bring back the happy atmosphere. Instead, I decide to go with something else. Something I think Kimberley will approve of just as much as if I'd made a joke.

"Ok, it's time to come clean," I say.

I glance at Kimberley, knowing that she'll know where I'm going with this. She gives me a little nod, letting me know she's good for me to tell them.

"Kimberley and I are giving things another chance."

The table erupts with everyone having something to say about it. I hold my hands up and wait until the questions stop.

"We're taking things slow, which is why we weren't going to say anything yet, because we don't want you all to make a big deal out of it."

"If that's what you want son, then it won't be a big deal," my mum says.

She beams at me as she says it and I can't help but laugh. The whole family are obviously pleased to hear that Kimberley and I are giving things another go. And I think I'm finally ready to forgive her for the past. I look at her and she smiles at me, her face flushed, happy.

When dinner is finished, Callie gets up and offers to start the dishes. Kimberley stands up saying she'll help her. Matt shakes his head and gets up.

"I'll help her. You just relax Kimberley. It's been too long since you were here, catch up with everyone. Make the most of it though. Next time you come, you're definitely on dish washing duty."

Kimberley laughs. We go through to the lounge where Kimberley entertains everyone with stories about the screw ups she made along the way at work before finally getting to where she is now. A lot of her stories are new to me too and I find myself relaxing and laughing along with everyone else. Matt and Callie come back in mid way through the stories.

"Does anyone want a cocktail?" mum asks.

"Not for me thanks," Kimberley says. "I'm driving."

"Get Sebastian to drop you off. Have a drink," Chance says.

"I'm happy to drop you off," I say.

Kimberley shakes her head.

"No honestly, I'm fine," she smiles.

I decline too as I'm driving. Matt and Callie came in a cab and Chance decides to leave the car. He goes off to make drinks for everyone else. I wonder briefly if I've upset Kimberley somehow; she seemed so adamant she didn't want me to drive her home. She launches into another story, and as she talks, she slips her hand into mine. Ok, I'm being paranoid. She's not upset with me, she just doesn't want a drink. I smile to myself. I'm acting like she's some kind of alcoholic or something. She's allowed to pass on a drink without me thinking I've somehow pissed her off.

We sit chatting for a bit longer. After a couple of hours have passed, Kimberley turns to me and smiles.

"I'm really hot. Do you fancy a bit of air?" she says.

I nod and get up and we excuse ourselves. I lead Kimberley through the conservatory and out into the back garden.

"Are you ok?" I ask her.

She smiles at me.

"Yeah," she says. "I was just a bit hot."

She takes my hand and we walk down the garden. The garden is big enough to get lost in. Large manicured lawns sprawl on either side of the winding path we walk down. Flower beds line it on either side and the air is alive with the scent of various flowers.

"I always loved your garden," Kimberley smiles. "We used to spend hours out here. Do you remember?"

"I remember," I say. "Oh my God, do you remember that night we decided to camp out here?"

Kimberley laughs.

"And it absolutely lashed down. How long did we last?"

"Less than an hour," I laugh.

I lead Kimberley onto a small gravel path that leads off the main path and take her through the shrubbery. It opens out on a clear area with a bench and a small creek trickling by.

"Remember this place?" I smile.

"Oh how could I forget it? It was our spot," Kimberley smiles.

We sit down on the bench, each lost in our memories. I remember Kimberley and I always used to come and sit on this bench and watch the sun go down together. We'd spend hours sitting here kissing, chatting laughing, planning our futures together.

The sun is beginning to go down now, casting long shadows over the garden, and creating a beautiful orange sky.

"I have a confession to make," Kimberley says.

I turn to look at her. She looks so beautiful. The setting sun makes her skin glow and the yellow shirt she's wearing makes her tan stand out.

"I wasn't too hot. I just wanted to come down to this spot and watch the sun set," she says.

I smile at her and then I lean in and cup her face with one hand. I push a lose strand of her hair back behind her ear and then I lean in and brush my lips against her. She shuffles closer to me and kisses me hard on the mouth. I run my hand through her hair, enjoying the silky feeling of it against my skin.

She pulls back slightly and smiles at me. I wrap my arm around her and she sits with her head on my shoulder as we watch the sun go down. I can't stop glancing down at Kimberley as she sighs with pleasure.

It's the perfect spot for a moment like this with the creek gently trickling by and the sun fading slowly away, making room for the night. I know that I'm falling in love with Kimberley all over again. I know I said I wanted to take things slowly, but I'm starting to regret saying that now. I just want to hold her in my arms and tell her I love her and that I never want us to be apart again.

I have to bite my tongue to stop myself from blurting it out and ruining the moment. I pull Kimberley closer to me and she snuggles against me, her hand on my knee.

"I love it here," she says.

"Me too," I agree.

It's the closet I can get to telling her I love her. I don't want to scare her away. But I don't know long I can spend with her this close to me without saying it.

We sit in silence for a while, a comfortable silence, broken only by the trickling of the stream. I realise that Kimberley is shivering.

"Do you want to go back to the house?" I say.

She nods her head.

"Why didn't you say you were cold?" I ask as we get up.

"I didn't want to ruin the moment," she smiles.

I laugh and pull her against my side as we walk. We reach the conservatory and I take hold of Kimberley's wrist, stopping her from going back in. She gives me a questioning look and I lean in and kiss her again.

"I just had to do that before we went back in," I smile.

She returns my smile and then she steps inside. I follow her and we go back to the lounge. Mum and dad are there, but Matt, Callie and Chance have disappeared.

"How come everyone's left so early?" I ask.

Mum laughs.

"Sebastian it's not early. You two have been out there for some time It's after eleven," she says.

I am shocked to discover we've been gone so long, but at the same time, I'm not surprised at all. Being around Kimberley, I've always lost track of everything else around me. It confirms what I already know. I am definitely falling back in love with her. She smiles up at me.

"We should go," she says.

I nod my head. We say our goodbyes to my parents and walk to our cars.

"Would you like to come back to my hotel?" she asks.

I nod my head eagerly.

"I thought you would never ask," I laugh.

"Well I don't want to be too forward. I have to keep you on your toes," she grins.

I get into my car and follow Kimberley in hers. Is it too early to tell her how I feel? Of course it is. It's been two weeks since we agreed to take things slow. And telling someone you're in love with them hardly counts for taking things slow.

I park my car beside Kimberley's in the hotel car park and hop out. We hurry up to her room and the door has barely closed behind us when we're reaching for each other, our lips coming together as clothes begin to fly. I wonder if being back in our spot had the same effect on Kimberley. If she's feeling like she's falling for me again too, or if she's just eager to have sex with me. I know she wants this to work. She said so herself. I should just tell her how I feel. But it's not something you blurt out during sex. Not unless you want to kill the mood completely, and I definitely don't want that. Kimberley's mouth on mine is setting me on fire, my cock standing to attention, ready to take her to paradise. No. I definitely don't want to ruin this moment.

Kimberley leads me towards her bedroom where we lose the rest of our clothes. She grins at me and kisses me again, walking me towards the bed as we kiss. Her hands are all over my body and mine are all over hers. I can feel her erect nipples against my chest.

We reach the bed and she pushes me backwards. I sit down hard on the bed and grin up at her. I reach for her and she shakes her head, dancing back out of my reach. She comes closer again and this time, I don't reach out for her. I've learned my lesson.

She stands between my knees, naked and sexy as fuck. She runs one fingernail down the centre of my chest and licks her lips. She gets to her knees and pushes my legs wider apart. She sucks my cock up into her mouth and begins to suck on it. Within minutes, I am fighting to control myself, holding myself back from coming as her expert tongue works my cock. Her hands roam over my thighs and stomach as she sucks me, sending goose bumps running over my skin. Not knowing where her hand will land next is tantalising as hell.

Finally, when I don't think I can hold myself back any longer, she raises her head and smiles at me, the smile of a seductress. She puts her hands on my shoulders and climbs onto the bed so she's straddling me. She leans forward and kisses me. I run my hands up and down her back, tasting myself on her lips.

She pulls back from our kiss and pushes me until my back is flat on the bed. She reaches behind herself, but before she can grab my cock, I flip her onto her back and kneel over her.

"Your turn," I say with a grin.

I move my legs so I'm kneeling between her spread thighs. I bend forward and run my tongue between her breasts. She arches her back, moving into my touch. I suck one of her breasts into my mouth, flicking my tongue back and forth across her nipple. I move to the other breast and run my tongue over her nipple until it's hard. I gently bite down on it, nibbling on her while my fingers probe between her lips and find her clit.

I wait until she's moaning and writhing, desperate for more and then I run my tongue down her stomach. I pull my fingers away from her clit and replace them with my tongue, eagerly lapping at her, drinking in her juices and savouring the taste of her. I suck on her clit, making her gasp out loud as her hips thrust beneath me. Her hands grab the sheet beneath her, balling it up in her fists as she moans long and low.

I keep working her, applying more pressure, pushing her over the edge. Her moan becomes a whisper, almost a whimper as her orgasm bursts through her, bringing her body to life. I keep licking her, moving her clit from side to side. She says my name over and over again, lost in a vortex of ecstasy as I run my hands down her sides.

She goes stiff beneath me, her head thrown back, her back arched. She makes a screaming noise, a primal noise full of lust and desire and I feel my cock pulse as I listen to her unearthly moans as I work her body. Her breath catches in her throat and she's silent for a moment, her mouth hanging open in a silent scream as I push her over the edge once more.

Her body relaxes, going limp as her pleasure overwhelms her. I kneel up, kneading her breasts and watching her as her eyes roll back in their sockets. They come back into view, and slowly, her vision returns to normal and she gives me a smile, biting on her bottom lip.

"Oh my God," she breathes. "I ... that was something else."

I lean forward and kiss her breastbone and then I lower myself on top of her. I enter her pussy, loving the way it grips my cock like a tight little glove. I begin to move, Kimberley moving with me. She bucks her hips, rolling me onto my back and she sits up, riding me. I move with her, enjoying the view as her breasts bounce wildly as she grinds herself onto my cock. I grab her hips and roll her onto her back and slam my cock into her.

She moans and grabs at my shoulders, my back, twisting my flesh as pleasure courses through her. Her pussy goes wild, clenching around me and I force myself to hold myself back. I don't want this to end. I kiss Kimberley's neck as I keep thrusting into her. I can feel her pulse racing against my lips. Her hands run down my back, and then back up again, like she can't bear to keep any part of her body still. She cries out as I pull almost all of the way out of her and then slam into her again. She screams my name as she comes hard, drenching my cock in her pleasure.

I have to bite the inside of my mouth to pull myself back from the edge. I can feel the pressure building inside of me, the desperate need for release filling me, but I can't let go yet. Kimberley's body is my playground, and playtime is far from over.

I keep thrusting as she clenches wildly around me, her breath coming in a series of ragged pants and moans as I keep going, pushing her over the edge time and time again. Her body responds to my touch, even as she whimpers. Her face is contorted, flushed red, sweat coating her upper lip. Her eyes are glassy with lust as she peers up at me, her mouth a silent O with her lips swollen and red.

I lean down and fit my mouth over hers, and even in her frenzied state, her mouth locks itself onto mine, her tongue tangling with mine. I want to devour her, to make her mine forever.

I up the pace of my thrusts, no longer able to hold myself back. I fill Kimberley with short, fast strokes that keep her gasping. When I finally let go and allow myself to come, I come hard, my cock rigid, spurting, pulsing into her. I feel my orgasm in my full body, a wave of pleasure that momentarily consumes me and I hear Kimberley's name being dragged from my lips in an animalistic growl. I bury my face in her neck as my orgasm floods me, making my skin tingle, my insides churn. I try to suck in a breath but I can't. Finally, the feeling starts to fade and I can breathe again. I suck in a gasping breath that sears my raw throat, a breath filled with scent of Kimberley.

Her arms are around my shoulders as she presses me against her as she too fights to breathe normally again. I stay in place, biting my tongue to stop myself from telling her that I love her.

Finally, I roll off her.

"Holy fucking shit," she laughs, rolling towards me.

I wrap my arm around her waist and pull her closer to me, still not feeling like I can talk yet. I just want to lay here beside her and hold her all night long. I can feel my eyelids growing as heavy as the rest of my body as I finally regain my senses. I let myself drift towards sleep with Kimberley in my arms.

❧

I wake up and yawn and stretch. I know instantly I am alone in the room. I can always sense Kimberley's presence when she's close to me, and although I roll over to check, I am right. I am in her bed alone. I stretch again and get up. I spot my boxer shorts on the ground and grin to myself as I remember last night. To say my orgasm was intense would be the understatement of the year. I pick up my boxer shorts and pull them on and then I head out of the bedroom to look for Kimberley.

It's immediately clear to me that she's not in the room. I shrug. Maybe she went downstairs to grab us some breakfast or something. I wander back out of the lounge area and go and take a shower. I get my clothes on and go back out to the lounge area where I see Kimberley still isn't back. I check the time. It's not even seven yet so there's no hurry to get to work.

I pull my phone out of my jacket pocket and go out onto the balcony. I sit down and check my emails. There's nothing that can't wait. My mind wanders back to last night. How I felt wrapped up in Kimberley, claiming her pussy, making her mine. It was a great night by anyone's standards, but I can't help but feel a little tug of remorse because I still didn't tell her how I feel. I am afraid to tell her. What if she doesn't feel the same way?

I pick my phone back up and I scroll through my contacts and find Matt's name. He likes to wind me up, but when it comes down to it, surely he won't take the piss about this. I hope not. I need his advice badly. I want to know how he knew it was the right time to tell Callie he loved her.

I make the call and he picks up within a couple of rings.

"How did you know when it was the right time to tell Callie you loved her without worrying it would scare her away forever?" I blurt out after Matt says hello.

"I didn't," he laughs. "I just kind of said it and worried about the consequences afterwards. Why?"

"Because I think I'm in love with Kimberley again and I'm afraid I'll end up blurting it out and ruining everything," I admit.

Matt laughs,

"For fuck sake Matt, can you just be serious for one goddamned minute?" I snap.

"Sorry," he says. "I'm not laughing at you for loving her, I swear. I'm laughing because you think this is new."

"What do you mean?" I say.

"You never stopped loving her Sebastian. I know it. Chance knows it. And somewhere deep down, you know it too. The only thing that's new here is you finally got your head out of your ass and are ready to admit it."

I ponder his words. Maybe he's right. Oh screw it, of course he's right. As if I would still have been bitter about Kimberley leaving all of these years later if it wasn't because I never really stopped loving her. I sigh.

"Ok, maybe you're right. Yeah, you probably are right. But that doesn't really help me any. How do I stop myself from blurting it out and ruining any chance we have of making this thing work?" I say.

"Seb, you have nothing to be afraid of. Kimberley loves you every bit as much as you love her," Matt says.

"How the hell can you possibly know that?" I say.

"Look, this merger. Yes, Kimberley took the idea to Joe Benton. Yes, it was a good opportunity and she did all of the leg work. But where do you think the idea came from?"

"She said she'd thought about it before and the time was right to act on it this time," I reply.

"Yeah. The time was right, because Chance and I went to see her and told her that we were sick of you moping around and asked her if there was any chance of you two getting back together."

"You did what?" I almost shout.

Matt laughs.

"Are you really mad about this?"

"No," I admit. "But I'd hardly say I was moping about."

"Well neither would I, but I figured telling Kimberley you were a serial flirt and fucked women you had no feelings for probably wouldn't have been the best way to get her to come back," Matt laughs.

I find myself laughing with him.

"Fair point," I say. "Was I really that easy to read?"

"Yes," Matt says without hesitation. "The only time you weren't obsessing over her was when you were neck deep in a work project. And Chance and I agreed that there's only room for one of us to be married to the job, and that's kind of his thing."

"So you're saying she came back because she loves me?" I ask, needing to be absolutely sure I'm not misunderstanding what Matt is saying.

"That's exactly what I'm saying. Now get your ass in gear, tell her you feel the same, and let her get settled. Seb she's living out of a hotel room because she doesn't want to get an apartment here until she's sure you really want more than just a fling with her."

I can feel my stomach churning, but this time, it's with excitement rather than fear.

"You're right. I'm going to tell her. Shit Matt, I'm really going to do this."

"Go get her bro," Matt says and then he hangs up.

I sit on the balcony a moment longer, smiling to myself. She never really did stop loving me. She was telling the truth.

I hear the door to the room opening and I jump up, full of nervous energy all of a sudden. I go into the lounge area, ready to whisk Kimberley up into my arms and spin her around. My excitement dies when I see her expression.

"What's wrong?" I ask, frowning with concern.

"Nothing," she says.

I move closer to her.

"Talk to me," I say. "Has something happened."

She steps around me.

"I said I'm fine," she snaps.

"Where have you been?" I ask, hoping to get some clue as to what could be wrong with her from where she's been.

"You should go or you're going to be late for work," Kimberley says, completely avoiding my question.

She doesn't give me a chance to respond. She disappears down the hallway and I hear the bathroom door open and then close. I frown. What the hell has gotten into her? It's like she was just dismissing me. I shake my head.

I'm not going to just leave until she tells me what's wrong so instead, I go over to the coffee making area and make us both a cup of strong, black coffee. I sit down and sip mine. It's gone cold before Kimberley is out of the bathroom and I'm starting to get really worried now. I get up and move down the hallway. I tap on the bathroom door.

"Kimberley?" I say.

No answer. I feel a knot of dread in my stomach and I knock louder.

"Kimberley? Answer me or I swear I'll break this fucking door down," I shout.

I can hear the panic in my voice as I shout.

"Relax Sebastian. I'm fine. Just go away," she says.

I can hear the tears in her voice. She's clearly not fine at all. I rest my forehead against the door.

"Please just tell me what's wrong," I say. "I can hear you crying."

She doesn't respond.

"Ok, tell me when you're ready," I say. "But I'm not going anywhere until you come out. If I have to sit here all day I will."

I mean it. I slide down the wall opposite the bathroom door and sit down to wait for her to come out. She's stubborn, but she'll have to come out eventually. God how did I go from being ready to tell Kimberley I'm in love with her to sitting on the ground listening to her crying and not even being able to hold her?

I don't know how long I've been sat here when the door finally opens and Kimberley emerges. Her face is blotchy where tears have run down her face. Her eyes are red. I push myself up to my feet, but Kimberley is already walking away from me.

"Kimberley, wait ..." I start.

I happen to glance into the bathroom as I get up and I see it in the sink. A pregnancy test. I walk into the bathroom and pick it up. One word sits there in the window. Pregnant.

My heart skips a beat and I feel my face breaking into a smile. It all makes sense now. Why Kimberley skipped the cocktails yesterday. Why she was evasive about where she had been this morning. Why she tensed up a little when my mum started talking about grandchildren. My smile dies on my lips when she speaks from behind me.

"Don't worry. I'm not keeping it."

"What? No. Kimberley wait, we need to talk about this," I say as she walks away from me again.

I chase after her into the lounge where she's already putting her jacket on.

"There's nothing to talk about," she says. "Except maybe how useless my contraceptive pill clearly is. You don't have to worry about it."

"Kimberley listen to me," I say. I take her hands in mine and wait until she's looking at me. "I love you. And I love that we're going to be a family."

She pulls her hands away and shakes her head.

"We're not going to be a family Sebastian. What part of this are you not understanding? I can't have this baby. I've never wanted one and I'm not going to have my career ruined now."

I can feel my mind whirling, dread filling my whole body. How can she be talking about killing our baby this way?

"Kimberley, stop," I shout. "You can't do this."

"Yes I can," she snaps. "My body, my choice. I know this has always been your dream. Getting me pregnant so I have to stay at home and play the good little wifey, but it's not going to happen. Just accept it."

I am floored by her words. I've never said a single thing to imply that's what I want. It's not something I've ever wanted. I've never wanted to hold Kimberley back and I don't want that now. What I want is for her to see that I love her more than anything and that we can make this work.

I'm not in right frame of mind to explain that to her though, and I know she's not in the right frame of mind to hear me. I head for the door.

"We'll talk about this later," I say.

"There's nothing to say Sebastian," she calls after me as I walk down the hallway to the elevator feeling like the bottom has just fallen out of my world.

Chapter Seventeen

SEBASTIAN

*J*t's been five days since Kimberley dropped her bombshell on me. Five fucking days of going insane. Five days of feeling as though the bottom is falling out of my world. It's like everything is spinning, like I'm screaming inside to get off the roundabout, but no one can hear me and the spinning never stops. I'm pretty sure this what the first step towards madness feels like.

I've tried calling Kimberley a few times, but she won't take my calls. I've left voicemails and sent text messages, but I get nothing in return. I've been up to her office just to be told that she's taken a few days off. I've even been by the hotel and knocked on her room door and called through to her, but if she's been in there when I've called round, she's ignored me.

It's like she's closed herself off to me completely. I'm not toob proud to admit it, but I've ghosted girls in the past, and it feels like that's what Kimberley is doing to me now. But she's carrying my fucking baby. She can't just shut me out like this. She can't. Except she can and she is.

I am completely torn up inside by this whole thing. It breaks my heart to know that Kimberley wants to get rid of our baby, and yeah, it pisses me off that she won't even sit down and have a conversation about it. I mean I get it – ultimately there's nothing I can do to stop her from having an abortion if that's what she wants to do, but she could at least hear me out before she makes such a big decision.

Yesterday, I sent Kimberley what I told myself would be my last text message to her unless she replied. It was a simple message telling her I understand that she's upset and that I'm here when she's ready to talk. I promised her that unless she reaches out to me, I'll leave her alone.

It's what I should do. She's shut me out and made it quite clear she has no interest in talking to me. The rational side of me is willing to accept that we gave it a go, and it's clearly not going to work out, despite my feelings for Kimberley. We're just too different. Kimberley runs from her problems and shuts herself off from the world, from me. I can't be with someone who leaves me hanging like that every time there's a problem. It's like a rollercoaster ride, but not a fun one. It's like riding a roller coaster with broken tracks and knowing the ride isn't going to end well, but not knowing for sure when the cracks will start to show, or when the track will just be pulled out from underneath you altogether.

The thing is, when it comes to Kimberley, I think it's fair to say that the rational side of me doesn't really get a look in. Already, I am itching to call her again, to text her, to make her talk to me. But I won't. I'm not some creeper guy who can't take a hint. And that's all there is to it. She's made her choice, and while I don't have to like it, I have no choice but to respect it.

I stand up abruptly. I have to get out of the office, get out of my head and get some fresh air, before I go completely mad. I need to be moving, to be doing something other than sitting staring at a blank screen and pretending to concentrate. If I'm doing something, anything, then I will be much less likely to cave in and break my word and message Kimberley again.

"Sebastian? Where are you going? You have a meeting in an hour," Bernie says as I leave my office.

I flash her a smile, hiding how I really feel.

"I'll be back by then. I just need to pop out for a moment," I say.

"Well what do you need? I'll get it for you," she says.

What I need is Kimberley to fucking talk to me. What I need is for her to hear me when I tell her I love her and we can be a family. I don't think Bernie can make that happen anymore than I can. I just shake my head. Bernie comes around the desk and puts her hands on my shoulders, forcing me to sit down. She goes back to her computer and types rapidly for a second and then she comes back around to me and perches on her desk and peers down at me.

"Something's wrong. Now spill it," she says.

"Nothing's wrong," I start.

"Yes there is. You were on top of the world last week, and now you're ... I don't know. Different. It's something to do with Kimberley isn't it?"

I feel myself nodding.

"Yeah. We gave it a go and it didn't work out. Don't worry, I've gotten over her once and I can do it again," I say.

Another lie. I never really got over her and I for sure don't think I can do it now. Bernie frowns and shakes her head.

"What is it you're not telling me? I've never seen you like this before," she says.

I open my mouth to tell her I'm fine, but instead, I blurt out the truth. As soon as the words Kimberley is pregnant leave my mouth, I feel better, and before I know it, the whole story has tumbled out of me. I haven't even told Matt or Chance about this. I haven't told them anything except sticking to the story that Kimberley and I are taking things slow. I even tell her what I've done – the grand gesture I was so sure Kimberley would love, but now seems ridiculous. God I'm such a fucking idiot. I can't believe I thought we could ever make this work. There's just too much history, too much mess.

"So yeah, there you have it," I finish.

"Oh Sebastian, I'm so sorry," Bernie says.

I shrug.

"I should have known better than to let her in again," I say.

"Just give her time. She'll come around," Bernie says.

"I'm not sure I want her to come around Bernie. I can't live my whole life like this with Kimberley shutting me out and blowing hot and cold on me."

"Then maybe it's for the best that you've found that out now rather than years down the line," Bernie says.

I nod mutely. I know she's right. It's better this way. But then why does it feel like my heart has been ripped out of my chest?

"Thanks Bernie," I say, standing up again. This time, she doesn't try to stop me. "And please keep this conversation between us ok?"

"Oh really? Because I really wanted to tell half of the office and a couple of clients about it," she says with a soft laugh.

I find myself laughing with her.

"Ok, point taken," I say. "I'm going to go and get some air and clear my head."

I glance at my watch.

"You better push that appointment back after all. Sorry."

Bernie grins.

"It's already done," she says. "I emailed him before I sat down."

I shake my head and laugh.

"What would I do without you Bernie," I say as I leave.

"Remember that next time pay rises are on the table," she shouts after me.

~

I've walked the streets around our office building for over an hour and I'd like to say I feel better, but I don't. I don't think I will feel better for a long time. But at least I haven't given in and called Kimberley so there's that.

I head back to the office with a heavy heart and a promise to myself to throw myself into work and forget Kimberley ever came back into my life. I cross the lobby and wait for the elevator. It comes and I step in.

"Hold the elevator please," I hear someone I shout.

I reach out and press the door open button and Joe Benton runs into the elevator.

"Thanks," he says. "How are you?"

"Good," I say. "You?"

"Good. We're getting settled in nicely and I'm finally starting to feel like we're organised," he smiles. "And who knows? I might even get home to my wife before she divorces me."

"That bad?" I ask.

He laughs and shakes his head.

"No, I'm just joking. She gets me. She knows I have to do this. And she takes all of her anger out on my credit card rather than me," he says.

I laugh with him and we fall quiet. I find myself thinking of Kimberley again, just for a change. This is my chance to find out how she's coping at least. She works pretty closely with Joe and if she's been acting weirdly, he'll have noticed. But if he knows anything, he'll think it's odd that I'm asking him about her rather than asking her myself how she's doing. Yeah, I'm just going to keep quiet.

"How's Kimberley?" I hear myself ask him.

Dammit Sebastian. Listen to the voice of reason for once in your damned life.

"Actually, she hasn't been feeling too well. She's taken a few days off to get herself put right," he says.

"Nothing serious I hope?" I say, knowing fine well there's nothing wrong with her.

She's just avoiding me and she doesn't want to risk running into me at work where she can't shut me out without risking me causing a scene.

"I think she's just a bit run down. The merger took a lot out of her, but she'll be back to fighting fit in no time. And after everything she did to make the merger run smoothly, she deserves a few days to recover."

I smile and nod my agreement.

"It's a shame she's moving on. I think she would have been great heading up this project," Joe says.

"Moving on?" I repeat.

Joe nods and smiles.

"Yes. She's not leaving the company, but she'll be going back to our London office. I can't say I'm ecstatic about it, but when someone with her skill set asks to move, you make space for her wherever the hell she wants to go," he says.

I nod, my head spinning. Kimberley's leaving? No, I must have misunderstood. She wouldn't just pack up and leave without even telling me. Would she? No. It must be a short term thing. But Joe didn't make it sound like a short term thing. I have to know for sure. We're almost at my floor and I turn to Joe.

"You mean she's asked to go back to London permanently?" I say.

"Yeah. It's what she wanted and like I say, you don't risk losing someone like Kimberley," Joe says as the elevator doors ping open on my floor.

I mutter my agreement and stumble out of the elevator. The doors close and it whisks Joe and his bad news back away. I lean against the wall for a moment. She's leaving me. Again.

I shake my head. I can't believe she's pulling this stunt yet again. I can't believe I was stupid enough to think she'd ever change. That she could genuinely put me before her career, or even have me rank equally to it.

I push myself off the wall and go back towards my office. I stop at Bernie's desk.

"She's leaving," I blurt out. "Running off back to London. I don't even think she was planning on telling me. Joe Benton just told me."

"So that's it then?" Bernie says.

I nod my head.

"That's it then," I confirm.

I go into my office and move towards my chair when it hits me. Kimberley is leaving me. For good this time. I stop before I reach my chair.

No. I won't let this happen. I told her I would never let her walk away from me again, not without a fight, and dammit, I'm going to fight for her. I'm going to put myself out there and risk getting my heart trampled on. I'll probably regret it. I'll probably come back broken and alone. But I'm going to do it anyway. I'm going to beg her to stay. I'm going to do whatever it takes to stop her from walking away from me. To stop her from getting rid of our baby. I turn around and leave my office again. Bernie looks up, surprised to see me leaving my office again so soon.

"I have to stop her," I say. "I swore to her I'd never let her leave again without a fight, and I meant it. I'm going to go to her and try to convince her we can make this work. I don't know if it'll make any difference, but I'm doing it."

Bernie grins at me, her face lighting up.

"That's more like it," she says. "I was starting to think you'd never get your ass in gear and fight for her."

"Can you do something for me?" I ask.

Bernie nods.

"Anything."

I write down an address on a piece of paper and hand it to her. I give her a small silver key.

"Can you go here and make sure everything's perfect?" I say.

She nods and beams at me.

"Consider it done. Now go get her."

For the first time since Kimberley dropped her bombshell on me, I feel alive. Like there's at least hope for us. I'm going to go to her and make her see that we can do this. That we can make it work. The three of us.

Chapter Eighteen

SEBASTIAN

I don't wait for the elevator. I'm too full of nervous energy to stand and wait for it. Instead, I take the stairs, running down them like my life depends on it. And maybe it does.

In my mind, I can see how this will go. I'll convince Kimberley to open the door, and I'll tell her I love her and beg her not to go. She'll step into my arms and tell me she'll stay, that she loves me too. And then we'll share the most magical kiss.

I don't know if that's really what will happen, but I have to hold onto that spark of hope. And whatever happens, I'll know I did everything I could to make this work. That I didn't let Kimberley walk away from me without a fight this time. I'll know that if she walks away from me again, that's all on her.

I practically sprint from the building and to my car. I drive to Kimberley's hotel sure I've broken every traffic law there is as I arrive there in record time. But none of that matters. All that matters now is getting to Kimberley and making her see how much I love her, and that we can handle anything together. I ignore the elevator in the hotel as well and take the stairs, sprinting up them two at a time.

I get to Kimberley's door and I knock gently at first. No answer. I bang harder. Still nothing.

"Kimberley? I know you're in there. I swear if you don't open this door, I'm going to break the damned thing down. I love you and I need you to know that. Please Kimberley, just hear me out," I say.

I keep knocking, pleading with her, but if she's in there, she doesn't respond. I stop for a moment and consider my next move. Am I really going to kick the door in? Yes, I think I am.

I reach for the handle, ready to press it down and kick beneath the handle. I don't have to kick it. It springs open when I push down on the handle. I grin to myself. Finally, something has gone right for me. I step into the room.

"Kimberley?" I call. "You might as well just come and talk to me because I'm not leaving until you do."

The suite has an empty feel to it, and I'm pretty sure Kimberley genuinely isn't here. I do a quick walk across the lounge area and down the little hallway. The doors all stand open and there's no sign of Kimberley. I shrug. It's not the end of the world. I can wait here until she gets back and then she'll have to talk to me. I know she hasn't left for London yet, or even moved on to a different hotel because I can see her jacket hanging on the coat hook and the bathroom still had her toiletries in it.

I go back to the lounge area and sit down to wait. I don't care if I have to wait here all day. If that's what it takes, then I'll do it. My cell phone buzzes and I pull it out. I have to do something to pass the time, so I might as well see who is texting me. Maybe it's Kimberley. Maybe she had the same epiphany moment as I did and raced down to my office and we missed each other.

It's not Kimberley. It's Bernie confirming everything is good at the place I sent her to, and telling me she's cancelled my day. I grin and text her back telling her she was right earlier. She does deserve a pay rise. And she's damned sure going to get one. She sends another text message telling me she'll hold me to that. I smile to myself, knowing she will.

I put my phone back In my pocket and get up. I can't sit still, I'm too full of nervous energy again. It feels strange being here in Kimberley's suite without her in it, but I tell myself it doesn't matter. Once I convince her to stay, she'll see the romantic side of me being here.

I go to the kitchen area to grab a coffee while I wait, and that's when I see it. A small white card, innocent looking but anything but innocent. I feel my heart lurch and my hand is shaking as I reach out and pick up the card.

It's an appointment card for a nearby family planning clinic. She's already booked the appointment to abort out baby. How could she? I look at the date and time and horror fills me as I see today's date. I glance at my watch. I have less than forty-five minutes to get to her and stop this.

I'm back off and running to my car, my heart pounding painfully in my chest. Each pulsing beat seems to mock me. There's no hope for Kimberley and I. She won't come around.

If she can do this to me, to us, kill our baby, then I know we're never going to be able to work this out.

I can't get her back. I know that now. But hopefully, I can still stop her from killing our baby. I drive to the clinic on auto pilot, ignoring the beeping horns, the shouted abuse, as I cut people off and narrowly avoid smashing into the car in front of me as it pulls in to park. I don't bother slowing down or gesturing angrily. What's the point? It doesn't matter anymore. Nothing matters except saving my baby.

I park in the clinic's car park, my car on an angle even a learner driver would be ashamed of. I don't care. I run into the clinic. I'm ready to demand Kimberley leave the clinic right now. I'll tell her I'll raise our baby alone if she really wants no part of this, and I'll tell her exactly what I think of her for attempting to do this behind my back.

I dash into the waiting room and feel a room full of eyes fall upon me. I barely notice them. I barely notice anything except Kimberley. She's sitting alone in the corner of the room. Her eyes are the only eyes that don't fall on me as I burst in. She's looking down at the ground, and I can see small wet spots appearing on her lemon coloured skirt as tears drip unwiped from her chin. She looks smaller somehow.

Looking at her like that, I know I won't yell at her. Or demand anything. Seeing her in so much pain hurts me physically. I can't make that pain worse. I won't. My plan gone, I no longer know what to say, but I feel myself walking towards Kimberley anyway. As I sit down beside her, she finally looks up. She's not wearing any make-up and she looks younger, more vulnerable than I've ever seen her. I reach out and wipe the tears from her cheeks.

"Sebastian. What are you doing here?" she asks in a small voice. "How did you even know I'd be here?"

"I went to your hotel room. The door was unlocked and I went in. I found your appointment card," I say.

She nods, not even angry that I invaded her privacy that way.

"Kimberley listen to me," I say. "I love you. Completely and fully. And I will be right by your side through all of this. Whatever you decide to do."

It hurts me to even think she might still choose to abort our baby, but I mean what I say. If she doesn't feel like she can be a mother, then who the hell am I to force that life on her? It will hurt to know that our baby is gone but it will hurt more to lose Kimberley.

She gives me a sad smile and I reach out and gently stroke her hair.

"Just promise me you'll stay here Kimberley," I say.

She looks down at her lap again and shakes her head.

"I'm sorry Sebastian. I can't do that," she says.

"Why not?" I demand. "You were up for us giving this a go. What changed?"

Her head comes back up sharply and she looks at me like I'm crazy.

"You really need to ask what changed? I got pregnant Sebastian. That's what changed," she says.

"I know. And I know that was never part of your plan, but it doesn't mean we have to be over," I say.

"Yes. It does. Because I'm not going to be one of those women," she says.

"One of what women?" I ask.

I'm starting to get really frustrated now, but I force myself to bite it back and be patient with her.

"One of those women who get pregnant and try to trap someone," she says.

"Ok, you've lost me. Why would you even think I would think that?"

"Sebastian you wanted to take things slow. And the second you saw that pregnancy test on the sink you said you loved me and we could be a family. I don't want you to feel like you have to pretend to feel something you don't to keep me happy. And frankly, I don't want to be with someone who is only pretending to love me because of some sense of honour or whatever. I get that I was just a fling to you – that's why you wanted to take it slow. And I can make my peace with that. But I can't make my peace with forcing you into something you don't want."

"Kimberley listen to me," I say, taking her hands in mine. "You're not forcing me into anything or making me feel trapped. I wanted to take things slow because I didn't want to let myself feel anything for you too quickly and get my heart ripped out again. But that didn't work did it? I told you I loved because I do. And I was going to tell you that the moment you walked through the door that morning, but I was too late. Look if you don't believe me, call Matt. I was on the phone to him before you got back and I told him I was in love with you, and I was afraid I would blurt it out and ruin things between us. He convinced me to just tell you how I feel."

"Really?" she asks, looking at me hopefully.

"Really," I confirm. "Kimberley I don't think I ever stopped loving you, even when I wanted to more than anything."

"Kimberley Montgomery," a nurse calls from the corridor opposite the waiting room.

Kimberley stands up and it hits me suddenly that if I let her go in there, we lose our baby. I meant it when I said I would stand by her side whatever she chooses to do, but I can't let her do this without at least trying to get her to reconsider. I can feel tears prickling at the corner of my eyes just at the thought of her going through with this. I jump up and catch up at her as she crosses the waiting room. I catch her wrist and turn her to face me.

"Kimberley wait," I say. "I meant it when I said I'll be by your side whatever you choose to do. And I will. But please, at least take a few more days to think about this. I ... please don't get rid of our baby."

She laughs softly, tears running down her cheeks at the same time.

"Sebastian I didn't want you to feel trapped or like you owed me anything. That's why I was leaving. But I'm not getting rid of the baby. This is just a routine check up."

"You ... you're not?" I say.

She shakes her head.

"No. I was in shock when I blurted that out. It's funny because I always said I didn't want children, but the second I found out I was pregnant, that changed. I felt a warm glow whenever I thought of the baby growing inside of me. And I knew I would never get rid of it."

"Ms Montgomery? Is everything ok?" the nurse asks, stepping closer to us, a look of concern on her face.

I realise I'm still holding Kimberley's wrist and I drop it from my grip. Kimberley smiles at the nurse through her tears.

"Everything's perfect," she says.

The nurse nods.

"Right this way then please," she says.

She turns and walks away and Kimberley starts to follow her. I stand on the spot and Kimberley looks back. She takes my hand in hers and pulls me forward with her.

"If you're going to be here every step of the way, you might as well start with the first step," she smiles.

I swallow hard, trying to get the lump out of my throat. I'm not completely clear on what will happen next, but Kimberley is going to have our baby. And it sounds like there's still hope for us.

I follow her through to the examining room. The nurse asks her a ton of questions and takes a urine sample and a sample of her blood. She smiles and says that she'll be in touch with the test results and she tells Kimberley to make an appointment for four weeks' time for her first scan.

"Where's your car parked?" I ask Kimberley as we leave the clinic.

"I walked here," she says.

"You walked here? Is that a good idea in your condition?"

She laughs.

"Oh God, don't turn into one of those types Sebastian. I'm pregnant not disabled."

"Sorry. This is just all kind of new to me," I say.

"And to me too," she smiles.

"Kimberley, can we talk?" I say.

She nods and lets me lead her to my car. I open the passenger door for her and although she rolls her eyes, she gets in without commenting. I go around to the driver's side and get in beside her.

"I meant it Kimberley. When I told you I'm in love with you. I really want us to make a go of this. If you still want to go back to London, I understand, but I swore to you I wasn't going to let you go without a fight this time, and I meant that too. So if you want to go, fine, but I'm coming with you."

Kimberley looks at me for a long moment, an expression on her face that I can't read. The silence stretches out between us and I want to say something to break it, but I don't know what to say. I'm starting to think Kimberley is going to say no. She's going to go back to London without me and I'm going to be one of those dads that misses his kid's first steps, first word. I'll get to see him or her the odd weekend and at school holidays and that'll be it.

"Kimberley, say something," I finally beg.

My words seem to break her out of her silent thoughts. She still doesn't say anything to me. She turns to face out of the front window of the car and she bends down and picks up her handbag. She pulls out her phone and scrolls through it.

"What are you doing?" I demand.

Is she seriously checking her emails in the middle of this? She holds up her hand and I am so shocked to see she's making a phone call now, in the middle of our conversation, that I fall into silence as she holds the phone up to her ear. Her other hand picks at her leg, removing imaginary fluff from her skirt. She won't look at me.

"Joe? It's Kimberley," she says finally. "About the transfer. Is it too late to change my mind?"

Warm relief floods my body at her words. She's still talking but I only catch a word or two here and there. Words like maternity leave. Pregnant. Baby. Less hours. She ends the call and finally she turns to look at me. She smiles.

"Does that answer your question?" she says.

"Yes," I say.

My insides are on fire as I look at this beautiful woman who looks back at me with love shining in her eyes. Have we finally done it? Have we finally got past the old problems and learned to communicate in a fashion? I think we have.

I lean forward and brush my lips against Kimberley's.

"I love you Sebastian," she whispers.

I kiss her with everything I have, using my kiss to show her how much she means to me, how I'll never let her go again. She shifts closer to me, wrapping her arms around me. It's kind of awkward hugging over the gear stick, but I hold her as tightly as I can, kissing her like I never want this moment to end. I can feel my cock responding to the closeness of Kimberley, but more than that, I can feel my heart responding to her.

I finally break the kiss and we look into each other's eyes. Kimberley is a little breathless and she smiles at me.

"Wow. I should have told you that sooner if it makes you kiss me like that," she smiles.

"I'll kiss you like that every damned day," I say.

Suddenly, something occurs to me.

"Wait. What did Joe say? Is it too late to cancel your transfer?"

She laughs and shakes her head.

"No. Joe never wanted me to leave here in the first place. He was only too happy to hear I'd changed my mind."

I grin, happier than I've ever been. I reach out and rub Kimberley's belly gently. I lean in and kiss her again. My lips have barely touched hers when she pulls away from me quickly. I barely have time to wonder what's going on before she spins in her chair and opens the door and retches. I hear vomit splattering on the ground. She wipes her mouth and pulls the door back shut, resting her head back against the seat.

"Ok. Maybe I won't kiss you like that again after all," I say.

She laughs softly.

"It's nothing personal. Just the baby letting me know he or she is awake," she says.

"Are you alright?" I ask.

She nods, but she's still a little pale.

"Yeah. I'm alright. Will you drive me back to the hotel please?"

Chapter Nineteen

SEBASTIAN

I reach across Kimberley and open the glove compartment of my car. I pull out a bottle of water and hand it to Kimberley. She smiles gratefully and takes the bottle. She opens it and takes a big mouthful, swills it around her mouth and opens the door again and spits it on the ground. She closes the door and opens the window half way down and then she sips the water, before she puts her head back against the seat and closes her eyes.

"Actually, there's something I wanted to show you. Are you up for it?" I ask.

Kimberley opens her eyes and looks across at me. I know she's going to say no and I try to swallow down my disappointment. I have to do what's right by her and if she doesn't feel up to this, then I will take her back to the hotel and we can go another time. But I so want her to see it. She's still looking at me and I think she can see the conflict on my face. Excitement at what I'm going to show her and disappointment that I'll have to postpone it.

"Sure," she says.

"Are you sure? Because if you don't feel up to it, we can go another time," I say.

She gives a soft laugh.

"I say yes and you try to talk me out of it?" she says. "Jeez Sebastian, learn when to shut up."

She's laughing as she says it and I do a quick salute and turn the engine on.

"Point taken," I say.

I pull out of the car park and start to drive.

"Like I said, I'm pregnant, not disabled, and I guess I had better start practicing what I preach," she says.

"Do you still feel sick like?" I ask.

She nods.

"I pretty much always feel sick. That's why I did the test. I was so sure I couldn't be pregnant with being on the pill and all, but I wanted to rule it out before I went to the doctor. The nurse said I'll feel better after my first trimester though."

"And that's when? Twelve weeks?" I say.

"Yeah. The end of week twelve," she smiles. "How did you know that?"

"Lucky guess," I grin.

"Rubbish. I didn't even think you'd know what a trimester way," she says.

"You're probably going to think this is weird, but I've been doing a bit of research. I read some books on pregnancy and what to expect. I figured if I could show you I was prepared for this then you wouldn't ... well you know."

She sits up straight and looks at me. I glance at her out of the corner of my eye.

"Seb I never should have even said I was going to get rid of the baby. I lied to you in there when I said it blurted it out because I was in shock. I mean I was in shock, but that's not why I said it. I was so sure you'd run a mile when you found out, and I didn't want you to think I was going to have the baby and you'd have to be a dad when you didn't want to be."

"Do you even know me at all?" I laugh. "I love the idea of being a dad Kimberley. I just didn't think it would ever happen because you were always so against the idea of having kids, and I guess I made my peace with it. I obviously did a good job of making it seem like I didn't want to be a dad though."

"You did. But if we're going to make this work, then you have to stop doing that," she replies.

"Well yeah obviously I'm not going to pretend I don't want kids once we have one," I say.

"That's not what I mean. I mean you have to stop lying to me about what you really want because you're scared I won't like the answer and you'll lose me."

I pause for a second. She's right and I know it. I was so afraid of her rejecting me when we were kids that I never really tried to get her to stay. And I have been so afraid of losing her since she came back into my life that I've been walking on egg shells instead of just telling her how I feel. Well that stops now.

"You're right," I say. "I promise that from here on in, I'll tell you the truth, even if I think you won't like it. But I need something from you in return."

She nods for me to go on.

"I don't feel like I can be open with you because whenever you think we're going to have a problem or you feel hurt, you push me away and you run from me. I need you to promise me that ends now. That if you're feeling scared or over-whelmed or hurt that you'll come to me and we'll talk," I say.

"It's hard for me to let my guard down and let anyone in," she says.

"No shit," I grin.

She gives a soft laugh.

"You think any of this came easily to me?" I ask.

She shakes her head and smiles.

"No. We're a real pair of fucking screw ups aren't we? I can't promise to be perfect Sebastian, but I can promise you I'll try. Can you live with that?"

I nod my head.

"Yeah. How about we both try and learn together that maybe it's ok to let someone in?"

"I like the sound of that," she smiles.

We fall back into silence. I keep sneaking glances at Kimberley as I drive. The colour is mostly back in her cheeks. Her skin looks healthy, glowing.

"So, where are we going?" she asks.

"It's a surprise," I say.

"Oh God, why does that make me nervous?" she laughs.

I would be willing to bet she isn't even close to as nervous as I am.

"Because you know I'm a little crazy," I say. "But don't worry. I cancelled the sky diving. I thought being pregnant and all, it wouldn't be the best plan."

"Oh don't even go there," she laughs.

When we've been driving for about half an hour, I pull into a quiet suburban neighbourhood and drive along a picturesque street. I pull up onto the driveway of a big white house. The garden is alive with flowers of every colour and Kimberley smiles as she sees the flowers.

I glance at her and she catches me looking at her. Her smile fades and she frowns at me, a questioning frown rather than an angry one.

"Who do you know that lives out here?" she asks, her tone suspicious suddenly.

I don't answer her question; I just smile at her instead. I get out of the car and before I can get around and open Kimberley's door for her, she's out and moving towards the front of the car where she meets me.

"Seriously, what are we doing here?" she says, peering around herself like she thinks the answer to that question might be written somewhere in the garden.

"It's one of Chance's design projects," I say. "I thought you might like to have a look around it."

"Ok," she says, drawing the word out and looking at me like I've lost my mind.

Maybe I have. But I sure feel good for a crazy guy.

"Come on," I say, holding my hand out to her.

Kimberley takes my hand and lets me lead her towards the house. We're almost at the door when she stops suddenly.

"Look I know you said it's a surprise, but I'll warn you now, if we go in there and a bunch of people jump out and yell surprise, I'm going to absolutely murder you. And I will make it a slow and painful death," she says.

Her face is deadly serious and I can't help but laugh.

"I promise no one will jump out on you," I laugh.

She doesn't look entirely convinced, but she starts walking again. I unlock the front door and push it open. I gesture to Kimberley to enter.

"After you," I say. "I don't want to ruin the moment when everyone jumps out."

She freezes and I laugh.

"I'm joking," I say.

She steps inside, her body tense, waiting for the yelling that of course doesn't come. She relaxes a little as I step in behind her and close the door. The foyer is open plan, all white, with a sweeping staircase running up the middle. A mahogany bannister matches the doors opening off the foyer and a small table stands at the bottom with a green potted plant on it.

"Don't be shy, take a look around," I grin.

Kimberley frowns but she goes to the first door and steps into a lounge. I hear her gasp as she looks around it. A cascading water feature takes pride of place above a huge mahogany mantelpiece. The gas fire is switched off, but when it's on, it casts soft shadows over the room with its dancing flames that make it look like a real fire. Brown leather sofas and chairs are arranged around a glass and chrome coffee table. Soft cream drapes hang at the window. Even I have to admit that Chance has outdone himself here.

"It's beautiful," Kimberley breathes.

I take her to the kitchen next. It's a strange mix of ultra modern gadgets placed in a farm house style room that really shouldn't work, but somehow it does.

"Oh wow. Look at this place. It's like a chef's dream," she smiles.

She has a similar reaction to the dining room and the library. Her face really lights up in the library, a bright, airy space lined with pine shelves, the centre of it filled with bean bags and a leather recliner.

"I could spend all day in here," she smiles.

Her face turns serious again.

"But seriously Sebastian. Why are we here?" she probes.

I don't reply. Instead, I leave the library and head back to the foyer. Kimberley follows behind me. I take her hand in mine, really feeling the nerves kicking in now. I lead her towards the stairs.

"I really do love you Kimberley," I say.

She pulls her hand out of mine, but she keeps following me up the stairs.

"Oh my God Sebastian. Is that why you've brought me here? Because I'll tell you now I'm not fucking in some random house," she exclaims.

Even though my stomach is swirling with nerves, I can't help but laugh at her indignation.

"It's not some random house," I say. "And we're not going to be fucking here. At least not yet."

We reach the top of the stairs and I lead her down the hallway.

"What do you mean not yet?" she says.

I turn back and take her hand again. She doesn't pull hers away this time and I take that to be a good sign. I hope she can't feel how sweaty my palm is against hers. My heart is racing as I push open a door.

"Come on, I want you to see this," I say.

I wanted to show her the master bedroom, the bathroom and the spare bedrooms first, leaving this room for the finale, but I can sense she's getting restless and I know she won't stop probing now until I tell her why we're really here. I don't want her to be pissed at me when she sees what I really want to show her.

I lead her into the room. It's all white with a border of yellow ducks around the centre of the walls. The floor is covered in a thick, soft white carpet. A white bassinet stands in the centre of the room, draped in voile that makes it look like it's right out of a fairy tale. Our fairy tale.

A white wardrobe and a matching chest of drawers stands off to one side of the bassinet, the handles finished in the same yellow as the ducks on the wall. A mobile hangs above the bassinet, a moon and seven stars hanging down from it. On the far wall is a changing station and a small bath. A wicker rocking chair sits in one corner beneath a shelf with books and alphabet blocks on it. A large cuddly duck sits in the chair.

"Do you like it?" I ask.

She nods, speechless as she looks at the room.

"Would it make a good nursery?" I ask.

She nods again. This time she gives a soft laugh and she turns to me.

"So that's what this is about. You're getting nursery design tips from Chance," she says.

"Actually, Chance designed the whole house except this room. This room was all me," I say.

"What? Why would you design a room for Chance?" she asks.

This is it. The moment of truth.

"Do you really like it?" I ask, ignoring her question.

"Yes, I love it. Are you thinking of switching career paths?" she asks.

I laugh.

"God no," I say. "But I'm glad you love it, because I've bought this house for us and designed this room for our baby Kimberley. If you're just saying you like it to make me feel better, then now's the time to be honest, because if you don't like it, we'll find a place you do like. I'll buy you any house you want and we'll do whatever you want with the nursery."

I know I'm babbling, but the nerves have well and truly gotten the better of me now Kimberley is standing before me and I'm telling her what I've done. It doesn't help that Kimberley's face is so damned hard to read. But as the saying goes, actions speak louder than words, and they certainly speak louder than a blank facial expression.

Relief floods me, turning my nerves to joy as Kimberley launches herself into my arms, wrapping her arms and her legs around me. She kisses me hard on the lips. I can taste the salt from her tears as I kiss her. We're both half laughing and half crying as we kiss.

Finally, I set her back down on the ground.

"I'm taking that as a yes to moving in with me," I say.

She raises an eyebrow.

"Umm, I said I love the house. And I do. But I don't remember you asking if we would be living together in it," she says with a teasing lilt to her voice.

She's grinning and I know she's just teasing me, but I'm still kind of a wreck when I ask her.

"Kimberley, will you move in with me?" I say.

"I'd love to," she smiles.

I kiss her again and I'm the happiest man in the world. I'm so glad I didn't let her run away from me again.

EPILOGUE

Seven Months Later

Kimberley

I can't believe how much everything has changed over the last seven months. Sebastian and I moved into the new house together and I absolutely love it. Not only is it amazing finally being able to put down some roots and no longer live out of a hotel room, but having Sebastian around all of the time is amazing. Being together all day every day has really brought us closer, and we're starting to open up to each other a lot more. And the sex. Oh my God, the sex. I feel like I've died and gone to heaven.

Eve and Carlton, Sebastian's parents, where over joyed when we told them the news. Both of us moving in together and of course about the grandchild they have on the way. Eve has bought us so much stuff that even if our baby wears each outfit once and never again, I don't think we'll get through it all.

Matt and Chance are still winding Sebastian up constantly, and he still bites every single time, but it's all in good fun.

Callie and I have grown really close too and I feel like I've gained a whole family rather than just a partner. Even Bernie has warmed to me. I think she can see how happy Sebastian is now we're together, and that's made her forgive me for the appalling way I treated her when she wouldn't let me into Sebastian's office that day.

"You ready?" Sebastian asks me with a smile as we get out of the car.

"Yeah," I laugh. "You make it sound like something I have to prepare myself for."

We're on our way up to Matt's apartment for brunch.

"You know what Matt and Chance are like," Sebastian says.

"They only wind you up. They're perfectly nice to me," I remind him.

"True," he grins.

We reach the apartment and step inside. Callie comes to greet us, wrapping me in a tight hug. Matt calls hello from the kitchen. Chance and Bernie are sitting at the dining table and they both shout hello as we go in.

"Where's mum and dad?" Sebastian asks.

"Dad got called away to deal with some emergency. It's in Paris so mum went with him."

"Lucky them," Sebastian grins. "When I get called to deal with a problem, it's in my own office building."

"Tell me about it," Matt says.

I walk over to the table and sit down beside Chance. Sebastian sits opposite me beside Bernie. Callie sits down and Matt finally begins bringing food to the table. He takes a seat as we begin to dig in.

"So Chance, you're letting the side down a bit now aren't you?" Sebastian laughs.

"What?" Chance says. "What do you mean?"

"You know, not having a significant other and all that shit. Matt and I are all grown up now and you're still playing the field."

"Playing the field? He doesn't even know what the field looks like," Matt joins in.

"Look just because you two are all loved up doesn't mean it's for me. I'm married to the job and I like it that way," Chance protests.

"He only says that because no woman in her right mind would have him," Matt laughs.

"That's a bit harsh," Callie smiles.

"Yeah, I mean look at you two and you both found someone daft enough to take you on," Chance shoots back.

"Hey," Callie and I chastise him at the same time.

"Just telling it how it is ladies," Chance laughs.

"Oh why don't we set you up on a blind date?" Callie says. "I'm sure I can find someone who would love a date with an eligible bachelor."

"Umm why don't we not," Chance laughs.

"Spoil sport," Callie pouts.

I feel a twinge in my stomach and I rub my hand over my bump.

"Are you alright?" Sebastian asks me with a frown, so in touch with me that he seems to know I'm in a little pain.

"I'm fine," I smile. "Just a little twinge."

"You're not going into labour are you?" Bernie asks.

I shake my head.

"No way. I've got another two weeks to go yet," I say.

"Well if you change your mind, can you have your waters break on the balcony? I've just had the floors cleaned," Matt says.

"Matt," Callie exclaims, giving him a dirty look.

"I'm joking Callie, relax," Matt says.

He looks at me and mouths I'm not. I laugh with them all, ignoring the pain in my stomach. It's just trapped wind or the baby sitting against a nerve in an awkward place or something.

I grab another pancake. I can't believe how hungry I suddenly am. Whatever is causing the twinges certainly isn't killing my appetite any.

Sebastian

*B*runch is almost over and we're starting to say our goodbyes. Kimberley excuses herself to go to the bathroom and I move over to get her coat from the chair it's draped over. Callie is putting some of the left over food into a bag for us to take with us. I shift from foot to foot wondering what's keeping Kimberley.

"Do you think you should maybe check on Kimberley?" Matt asks.

"Do you think she's been gone a long time too?" I say. "I thought I was just being paranoid."

Matt nods and I move through to the hallway. I tap on the bathroom door.

"Kimberley? Are you alright in there?" I shout.

"Ummm yeah. But Matt might not be too pleased with the puddle on his floor," she says.

"You're in labour?" I say.

"I hope so. Because if not, I've peed myself," she says.

I feel a mixture of excitement and panic fill me.

"Open the door," I say.

"It's not locked," she says.

I push the door open. Kimberley is sitting on the closed toilet lid, her hands pressed to her bump. She gives me a nervous looking smile.

"I'm scared Sebastian," she says.

"You don't have to be scared. I'm right here. Let's get you to the hospital."

I help her up and wrap my arm around her waist.

"Is it happening now?" Callie asks as we step back into the lounge area.

I nod, barely able to keep the grin off my face.

"About your floor ..." Kimberley starts.

Matt waves her words away with a laugh.

"I was joking, really. It'll wipe up." He turns to me. "Do you need a ride to the hospital?"

"No it's fine. I have my car downstairs."

Kimberley moans beside me and bends double as a contraction hits her. She breathes through it as I stand watching, feeling completely helpless. She straightens back up again with a relieved sigh when it passes.

"They're less than four minutes apart now Seb. This is moving quickly. And we need to move quickly too," she says.

I don't wait around when she says that. I whisk her out of the apartment with promises to call Matt the second the baby comes. I practically run her to the car and head straight for the hospital.

Luckily, the roads are clear and the hospital isn't too far away, but by the time we get there, Kimberley's contractions are only two minutes apart and she's really starting to freak out.

"It's ok," I reassure her. "We're here now and before you know it, our baby will be in your arms."

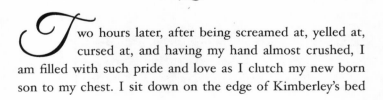

wo hours later, after being screamed at, yelled at, cursed at, and having my hand almost crushed, I am filled with such pride and love as I clutch my new born son to my chest. I sit down on the edge of Kimberley's bed where she lays looking exhausted but happy. I smile at her and she smiles back at me.

"He's perfect," I whisper.

"I know," she smiles. "He looks just like you."

I laugh and shake my head in wonder.

"So, what are we going to call him. I don't think Aria really suits him do you?" Kimberley grins.

I laugh and shake my head.

"Nope," I say. "Why were we both so sure he was going to be a girl?"

"I have no idea," Kimberley grins. "We really should have found out the sex when we had the chance. You're not disappointed are you?"

"Disappointed? No of course now. But I have no idea what we should call him."

"I did have one idea," Kimberley smiles. "I was thinking maybe Carl. You know, after your dad."

"He'd love that," I smile.

"Carl it is then," she smiles. "Carl Hunter."

"You know, if he's going to take my name, maybe you should too," I say.

"Why Sebastian, are you proposing to me?" Kimberley smiles.

"I know it's the worst proposal in the world, and I don't even have a ring yet, but I don't know. It just feels right. Yes, I'm proposing to you. Kimberley, I love you. Will you marry me?"

"Yes," she smiles, and for the second time that day, she makes me the happiest man in the world.

The End

COMING NEXT

Tangled With The CEO

CHANCE

I raise my glass in the air as the others do the same and then I down my rum. I get up and go to the small bar at the back of the plane and pour another one.

"Careful Chance," Sebastian warns me with a laugh. "You might actually start enjoying yourself."

I laugh along with the others, but Sebastian is right. I have a few things to do before I can let my hair down and enjoy myself this weekend. I take my drink back to my seat to sit down and watch the others for a moment.

Matt and Sebastian, my two older brothers, are playing some sort of drinking game, cheered on by Bradley, Mark and Rick, Sebastian's friends. It's his stag night and we're on our way to Vegas. I know I should be making more of an effort, but I just can't get in the mood until I know the few loose threads I had to leave at work are tied up.

In some ways, I admire Matt and Sebastian. They work hard, but they play hard too, especially Sebastian, although he's calmed down a little since he became a father. Carl is almost two now and fatherhood suits Sebastian in a way I never thought would be possible. I half wish I could be a little bit more like Matt and Sebastian. Just leave my work at the office and worry about it on Monday. But it's just not my style.

I'm not the sort of guy who can put off things that need to be done. They only play on my mind and niggle at me, where as if I can just get them done, then I can stop thinking about them. Except one thing always leads to the next and then I start thinking about that. And so it continues until my day off becomes another work day.

I sigh and shake my head. I don't know why I'm suddenly being so reflective. I like my life. I like being all about work. I love what I do and it's going to take more than a few nights in Vegas to convince me that I'm missing out on something more.

"Hey Chance?" Matt says.

I look up.

"It's a stag party, not a funeral. Smile or something." He laughs.

"Isn't it pretty much the same thing?" I ask. "Once Seb gets married, his life is pretty much over right?"

This gets a chorus of cheers and a laugh from Sebastian.

I grin and tell myself to forget work, just for a couple of days while we have the stag party and then get the wedding over with. I can always catch up on work and now isn't the time for work. It's the time to be a good brother. I get back up to join the others where they're still crowded around watching Matt and Sebastian play their drinking game.

It's a good thing we have a private jet, because I don't think a standard airline would take too kindly to this game. The only rule seems to be to sink as many shots as possible.

"What are they playing?" I ask, taking in the piles of shot glasses and the bottle of half gone Tequila.

Mark laughs. "I don't think it has a name. Maybe it should be called alcohol poisoning or something. They have to build a pyramid out of shot glasses. The first person to do it wins and the other one has to drink five shots of Tequila in a row."

It didn't look quite as lethal as I first thought, now I know most of the shot glasses are just being used as building bricks.

Matt puts his hands in the air and cheers when he sets his final shot glass on his pyramid and it doesn't fall over.

Sebastian groans. "Remind me again, why I suggested playing this. I suck at it." He laughs.

"Shut up and drink." Matt chuckles.

Sebastian shakes his head. "I've already lost two rounds. I won't see Vegas at this rate."

"Drink, drink, drink," the guys begin to chant.

I find myself joining in with them.

"Okay, okay." Sebastian grins, holding his hands up in surrender. He downs the shots one after the other, wincing after each one. He gets to the last one, looking like he's about to throw up. He chases it down with half a bottle of beer and moans loudly when he's done.

This gets him a round of cheers from the guys. He gets unsteadily to his feet and stumbles towards the bathroom.

An even louder round of cheers rises up with some laughter and clapping. It's obvious what he's going to do as he disappears into the bathroom.

Matt gets up and puts his fists in the air. "Reigning champion. Who's next?"

"Me," I say, surprising myself.

"No way!" Matt scoffs. "You'll be able to have the pyramid built in seconds. You do this all day every day."

"I'm an interior designer." I laugh. "What part of that involves building pyramids out of shot glasses?"

"Ah, you know what I mean." Matt grins. "Building stuff, designing stuff. It's all the same thing isn't it?"

It's not even close and I doubt for a second I would beat Matt at building the pyramid, but I'm not bothered about winning. I just want to get a bit tipsy and get into the same high spirits the others are in. "Okay." I grin. "How about we just pretend we played and you won and I'll drink the shots?"

"Really?" Mark says, raising an eyebrow.

"Really," I confirm as I sit down.

Bradley grabs five shot glasses and begins to fill them up with Tequila. He's onto the fourth one when Sebastian comes back out of the bathroom.

He still looks a little bit white, but he looks a damned sight better than he did before he went into the bathroom.

"Are you okay?" Matt asks him.

Sebastian laughs and nods. "Tactical heave. Bring it on." He picks up his half empty bottle of beer and starts drinking again, barely even slowed down by his throwing up. He spots me sitting at the table with the shots in front of me. "Wait. You played?"

"No," I say shaking my head. "The reigning champ here was afraid to take me on. So, I thought I'd just down the shots." I didn't wait for Sebastian's reply. I pick the first shot up and down it. The Tequila tastes pretty awful, bitter, but I swallow fast and feel the warmth as it spreads through me. I chase it down with the next one and the next one until I've drained all five. I smile up at the others.

They are watching me in a state of shock.

"What?" I ask.

Rick laughs. "You didn't even flinch."

"You said you couldn't drink shots," Mark adds. "But seriously, you're on fire."

I correct him. "I said I don't drink shots. Not that I *couldn't*." Considering how little I go out, I actually have a surprisingly high tolerance for alcohol, I just don't like drinking shots. It seems so frat boy. Immature and not my style at all.

"Chance's way too grown up for shots." Sebastian chuckles. "He'd much rather have a good glass of red wine."

Actually, I'd rather have a good glass of rum or brandy, but he's not completely wrong.

"Yeah, a stag night is kind of wasted on Chance," Matt agrees.

"You don't say," I agree. "I did say I would be perfectly happy not to come."

"Don't start with that shit again." Sebastian laughs. "We're family. That means you have to show up."

"I did show up," I remind him. "But you can't pull the family card. You let Dad off the hook."

"Well yeah, because he's Dad," Sebastian replies. "You really think he'd follow the *what happens in Vegas stays in Vegas* rule? He'd spend the next lord knows how long reminding us of every stupid thing we say and do tonight."

"True," I say.

"Anyway, Vegas is hardly Dad's scene is it?" he adds.

"It's hardly my scene either," I say.

"Yeah, but you only think you're ancient and past it. You're twenty-four, start acting it." Matt laughs.

I snap. "Just because I'm the youngest, doesn't mean I have to be the dumbest." I realize I've made everyone feel awkward as I snap at Matt. "You know being the dumbest is Sebastian's thing. This is his night, so let's not try to take his title," I say with a grin, quickly turning the mood back around to laughter.

"You haven't seen anything yet. Wait until we hit the strip tonight and you'll see just how dumb I can be," Sebastian agrees.

This gets another round of cheers and another cry for shots.

I resist the urge to roll my eyes, reminding myself this is Sebastian's night not mine, and when a shot of something neon blue is handed to me, I don't resist. I tell myself I can do this. I can be the fun one for a few days. God, people do much worse things for much longer periods of time. Going to Vegas for a few days partying is most people's idea of fun and here I am on a private jet going to stay in a nice hotel and I'm acting like I'm on death row or something.

We down the shots and the conversation moves on to the night's plans. And they say I'm the boring one. Who plans a night in Vegas? You leave your hotel, follow the lights and go with the flow. That's really what Vegas is about. Living in the moment. Being a bit reckless and doing something you wouldn't normally do.

My work phone vibrates in my pocket and I move away from the group to go back to my seat, pulling it out. I glance at the screen and roll my eyes. It's Dennis Rogers. I'm doing a full redesign for his holiday home. The plans are all done and he doesn't want the work to start until the back end of next week, and yet he's never off the phone with me. I debate ignoring his call, but I know if I do, I'll only spend the rest of this week thinking about what he wants until I call him back on Monday. I take the call.

"Mr. Rogers. Is everything okay?" I ask.

"It's Dennis," he reminds me. "And yes, everything's fine. Or at least I hope it is. I got a call from a contractor this morning about them wanting to be in the house next Wednesday afternoon. I'm not leaving until Thursday morning and I've told them that won't work, but they said they had your permission?"

"Yes. It's just what we discussed. They won't be starting any of the work. They just want to come out, get the keys from you and have you show them how the security system works. Remember? You said Wednesday would be the best day for you?"

"Oh. Yes, of course. I remember now. Sorry to have bothered you," he says.

"It's fine, really, you haven't bothered me," I lie.

"Oh. There's just one more thing," he says.

"Go on," I say through gritted teeth. Before he can respond, my phone is being snatched away from my ear.

Sebastian grins down at me with my phone in his hand.

I glare at him.

He ignores me as he looks at my phone and then puts it to his ear. "Hi, Mr. Rogers. This is Sebastian Hunter. Chance is actually taking the rest of this week off for a family thing, and he'll call you on Monday." He ends the call.

"What the fuck? That was a client," I snap, angry now.

"I know. Mr. Rogers. And you can tell him on Monday what an asshole I am. But for now, you can forget about him, forget about work, and have a good time. You were doing so well there for a moment."

I roll my eyes and hold my hand out for the phone.

Sebastian holds it out of my reach, mocking me. "Seriously Chance, you promised you wouldn't be working through my stag night."

I continue to glare at him but it has no effect on him whatsoever. I sigh. "I told you I wouldn't work while we're in Vegas. And we're not in Vegas yet."

"That's a technicality and you know it," Sebastian counters.

His little game is starting to piss me off now. Of course, I want him to enjoy his stag night but I honestly think he can have just as good a time if I take a phone call. He'd probably have had a better time if he'd just listened to my protests and let me sit this one out.

I snatch for my phone but Sebastian sees me coming and whips it back out of my reach. He throws it to Matt who catches it with one hand and promptly dumps it in a pitcher of water.

"For fuck sake!" I snap. "Have you two got no sense between you or what?"

Matt just laughs. "It's only your work phone," he points out. He peers down at the water. "It's not even your current one. Just have one weekend where you're not working. Is that really too much to ask?"

It probably isn't. It definitely isn't. But the point Matt and Sebastian are missing is that I want to work. I'm not doing it because I think the world will stop turning if I take a couple of days off. I'm doing it because I enjoy it. I like to be kept in the loop. Trying to explain this in a way that doesn't make me sound like I've lost the plot, isn't going to be easy though and I just shrug. "Fine. Whatever. You've made the decision for me now, haven't you?" I get up and turn towards the bathroom.

"Chance, wait," Sebastian says.

I turn around, stupidly thinking he's going to apologize, but then I see he's grinning.

"Matt said that's not your current work phone. Hand it over." He holds his hand out.

"So, you can put it in a jug of water? I don't think so," I reply.

"I swear I won't," he says. "I'll put it somewhere safe until after the weekend." His hand is still out and he's blocking my path.

I know it's going to be pointless to argue with him, so I take my other phone out of my pocket and slam it into his hand.

He pockets it and keeps his hand out, raising an eyebrow at me.

I sigh and pull out the third and final phone and give him that too. "If you think you're getting my personal phone, then you're very wrong," I say.

He grins and shakes his head. "Nah, you can keep that one. It's not like you have a hip and happening social life, where you'll be getting calls on that one is it?" He laughs.

I shake my head in annoyance and storm away from Sebastian and his stupid taunts. I lock myself in the bathroom, put the toilet lid down and sit on it for a moment. God, why can't I just be normal and enjoy a boozy weekend with the guys?

I stand up and wash my hands in cool water. I tell myself that's exactly what I'm going to do. Right after I get to the hotel, sort Mr. Rogers' problem out and deal with a couple of other things.

CHANCE

When we arrive at our hotel, we agree to all go up to our rooms, freshen up and meet back in the lobby in two hours. Two hours sounds like an awfully long time to me and I think Sebastian secretly wants to take a nap before we head out, but I bite my tongue. It will give me time to get things in order and make a few calls from my room before we go out. And then I can keep my promise to Sebastian and stop working.

If he hadn't acted like an ass on the plane and took my phones away my work would be done now, but then lord knows, how I would have filled the next two hours.

My room is on the eleventh floor and I step out of the elevator into a nice, clean looking hallway. The walls are painted off white and the flooring is a thick red carpet. Gold light fixtures are set at even spaces along the way. The gold is a little gaudy in my opinion, but hey, it's Vegas and that's Vegas isn't it? Over the top, gaudy, cheesy. But a good night out.

I reach my room and step in. The room itself is nice and elegant looking. A large bed with a pristine white duvet takes center stage in the room. A black runner sits about three quarters of the way down it. There's a black leather sofa beneath the window with a small table beside it. The wardrobe is a built in one with mirrored doors, and there's a pine chest of drawers and bedside cabinets. Opposite the bed is a large desk with a TV on one end and space to work at the other. I grin to myself when I spot the phone. That will stop me from having to use my personal phone and risk clients getting my personal phone number.

I peer into the bathroom which is all tiled in white with the occasional black one scattered in that breaks up the white and stops the room from looking too clinical while maintaining the clean, pristine look they'd been going for. There's a large double shower and a Jacuzzi bath, both of which look shiny and clean.

As rooms go as opposed to suites, I've stayed in much worse. I open up my suitcase and quickly unpack my stuff. I find a pair of fluffy white robes hanging in the wardrobe. When I've finished unpacking, which takes less than ten minutes, I go into the bathroom and strip my suit off. It feels good to finally lose the suit as it's so hot out here. I take a shower and go back to my main room.

I get dressed for tonight in a pair of black ripped jeans and a pale blue t-shirt. I run my hands through my hair, mussing it up a little and add a spritz of Armani and I'm done. A full thirty minutes after arriving at the hotel.

I go to the mini bar and grab a rum. I add a couple of ice cubes and take it to the little table beside the leather sofa. I pick the phone up and move it to the small table. The cable just reaches and I grin to myself. Something had to go right for me work wise.

Before I begin working, I sit down and sip my rum, looking out of the window. I have a fantastic view of the strip and even though it's barely started to get dark, lights flash everywhere. It really is the perfect place for a stag night and as I sip my drink, I promise myself that once we get out tonight, I will forget about work altogether.

The decision made, I pick the receiver up, dial nine for an outside line, and call the office. I get the phone numbers I need and program them into my personal phone when I realize I don't have anything to write them on.

I call Dennis Rogers back first.

"Chance?" he says, surprised when I tell him it's me. "Your brother said you were taking the weekend off."

"Please excuse Sebastian," I say with a laugh. "It's his stag party and he's a little out of control."

"You're at his stag party and you're working? Seriously, this can wait until Monday. Have a great time and have a drink or two for me." He ends the call before I can argue with him.

I frown a little. Even my clients are telling me to ignore work for a few days. If only it was that simple. I shake my head and smile to myself. If I'd spent my time slacking off, partying and dating, then I wouldn't be where I am now. I joined the firm straight out of college and I've worked my ass off ever since to prove that I'm the best at what I do in the city.

I think I've proved that. My clients always come back to me, and my services are booked in advance for the next year. I know deep down I have nothing else to prove and I know if I took a step back, the talented designers who work alongside me would be able to do a great job, but it's just not me. Why would I have worked so hard to get to where I am if I just wanted to slack off and hand my work off to others? If that's all I'd wanted to do, I could have taken a more corporate role but the thought fills me with horror. Being stuck in an office all day and never getting to do anything creative is my idea of hell.

I make a few more calls and then I check the time. I have about twenty minutes before I have to meet the others and I pick the phone back up to make one more call. I listen to it ringing and then a female voice asks how she can direct my call. I give her my name and the name of my client and she asks me to hold for a moment. Dreadful hold music fills my ears.

My hotel room door bursts open and I glance up in annoyance as Sebastian comes bounding in, calling my name. I cover the mouthpiece of the phone in case my call goes through and hiss at Sebastian to shut up.

He just laughs. He comes further into the room and shakes his head when he sees me on a call. He marches to the desk and bends down. He sticks his hand behind the desk and the line goes dead in my ear. Sebastian straightens back up and grins at me, showing me the cord he's just disconnected from the socket.

I slam the receiver down and get to my feet. I'm taller than Sebastian and I stand over him, glaring at him in frustration and anger. "What the fuck are you playing at Sebastian?" I demand as I step closer to him, my anger showing.

Sebastian ducks out of my way, but he's still laughing and waving the cord, taunting me. It's like he wants me to punch him or something. "Relax Chance. You're more uptight than

Dad. I know you think Kimberley and I won't last, but I'm telling you, she's the one, and—"

"What makes you think I think you and Kimberley won't last?" I interrupt him.

"Because I've spent so long playing the field," he says.

"Only because you were trying to get over her in the first place," I say. I know that's not the real reason he thinks that. I can see it on his face. I rack my brains, trying to think of anytime I've said something that he could have taken to mean I thought him and Kimberley were doomed. I can't think of anything. "Come on Seb. Why do you really think that?"

"Well, the whole love and marriage thing isn't really your thing is it?" he says.

"Not at all," I agree. "But that doesn't mean I think it's not for everyone. You and Kimberley are made for each other."

"So, why aren't you taking this seriously then?" Sebastian demands. "I'm only ever going to have one stag party and you can't stop working two fucking days for it?"

Maybe, he has a point. Yeah, he does. But that doesn't excuse him cutting off one of my calls not once, but twice today. He had no idea who those calls were to, and even once he saw my client's name on the screen on the plane, he had no idea how he would react to being essentially told to fuck off. He could have cost the firm a lot of business.

"Fine. I'll stop," I say.

"Good." He grins then shakes his head. "I honestly can't believe we're in Vegas and I'm having to impose a no working rule. The hard part should be convincing everyone it's over and they have to go back to work."

"Whatever. I've told you I'll stop. Now, do me a favor, and stay the hell out of my room, otherwise you're not going to live long enough to marry Kimberley."

"Ooh, fightin' words." Sebastian grins. "Bring it on, bro." He's dancing around the room, his fists up.

I try to stay mad at him, but I'm laughing at his antics.

"Ah see, you can smile without your face breaking," he teases me and stops dancing around. "We're going to have a couple in the hotel bar before we head out. Are you ready?"

Before I can answer, Matt steps into the room. "Why is Sierra downstairs in reception?" he asks me.

Fucking hell. This is just getting worse. She was meant to sneak in without either of my brothers or Bradley seeing her.

Both Matt and Sebastian are staring at me now, their eyes burning a hole into my guilty face, waiting for an explanation.

"Look, I agreed not to work for this weekend. But that doesn't mean shit can just be left to not get done. Sierra will be taking care of a few things for me while we're here, that's all," I say.

"It takes your work obsession to a whole new level when you can't go on a stag night without bringing your assistant along." Matt smirks.

"I'm glad you think this is funny," Sebastian says. "Do you have any idea how much trouble I'm going to be in now?"

I narrow my eyes at him. "You think Kimberley will be jealous because Sierra's here?" I ask.

He laughs and shakes his head. "God, no. But Bernie will. She's pretty much my best friend and I told her she couldn't come out here with us because it's a guy thing. She got it, but it'll be a whole different ball game if she finds out about this."

"It's not like she's here for the party," I defend. "And besides, hen parties are always rowdier than stag parties. She'll have a much better time with the girls."

He shrugs. "Just make sure you tell her I had no idea about this if she finds out," Sebastian says.

"I will. I'd better go and find Sierra and see what's taking her so long. I just have to quickly go through what I need her to focus on and I'll meet you two in the bar in ten." I grab my room key, phone and wallet and leave the room, reminding them to flick the lock over when they leave. I walk away knowing they're both staring after me.

I head down to the lobby, quietly fuming. I'm annoyed at my brothers; they don't want to work this week, yet they don't seem to want anyone else covering the work that needs to be done either. I'm still annoyed at Sierra too. I mean how hard is it to be in a place the size of fucking Vegas and not get seen by the few people who would recognize you?

I step out of the elevator and cross the lobby.

Sierra is just turning away from the check-in desk. She's wearing a sensible knee length pencil skirt with a white blouse and a black jacket. If she's too hot, she's not showing it. Her ashy blonde hair is clipped up in a French pleat. She clacks across the lobby in her heels.

"Sierra," I shout.

She turns to face me. Her perfect posture doesn't falter, but she gives her nerves away by pushing her glasses up. Something she always does when she's nervous. She comes to stand before me. "I'm so sorry Mr. Hunter," she says. "I checked the lobby before I came in, but then there was a problem at the desk and it took longer to sort it out than I thought it would, and then Matt was there. I tried to lie to him, but he saw straight through it. Have I caused a whole lot of trouble?"

I can feel some of the anger leaving me. Sierra has been my assistant for the last two years, and this is the only mistake I can ever remember her making. If this is as bad as it gets, then we're all good.

I shake my head. "No, I'll handle it. Now what was the problem at reception?" I ask.

"They said they couldn't find a room booked for me. I had to beg them to let me go up to your room and find out what was going on. They only agreed because I showed them my company ID and they recognized your name," she says.

"Wait here. I'll fix it," I say. I go up to the desk and flash a smile at the receptionist there. "My name's Chance Hunter. I have two adjacent rooms booked for this evening and tomorrow evening. My assistant has just tried to check into hers and she was told there's no record of her having a room booked here."

"Let me check that for you, sir. Chance Hunter you said?"

I nod.

She starts clicking on her keyboard. She gives me a professional smile. "I see the booking here." She makes another few clicks. "Oh, I see the problem. Because you had already checked in when your assistant arrived, the booking moved to another part of the system. I'm sorry. My colleague is new and wouldn't have known to check there."

"No worries," I say.

She hands me a key card and wishes me a pleasant stay.

If only she knew. I turn back to Sierra.

Rick is talking to her and as I get closer, I hear their conversation.

"So yeah. I'm in room 217 if you want some company later," Rick says.

I see Sierra tense up as she shakes her head. "As I said, I'm here for work. And I don't know if that line has ever worked for you before, but I can assure you it wouldn't work on me even if I was here for pleasure."

I shake my head and shove Rick away from her.

He frowns at me. "What? I can't talk to women now?"

"You can talk to women all you want, just quit harassing this one. This is Sierra, my assistant," I say.

"Oh. Sorry," he says. He winks at Sierra. "You can't blame a guy for trying, can you?"

She smiles and shakes her head.

Rick wanders over to join Mark.

"Sorry about that." I hand her the key for her room. "Your room is 1124. It's next door to mine, so if you need anything, you know where to find me. Did you bring the Bramer files like I asked?"

She nods her head.

"Good," I say. "He has some rather bizarre requests as you'll see. It could take weeks to source some of that stuff, so if you can make a start on going through it all, that would be great. I also need you to arrange a meeting with Vince Falcrow. Oh, and can you send Dennis Rogers something. An apology for Sebastian cutting off our call earlier. I've spoken to him since and he's fine about it, but it won't hurt."

"Got it," Sierra says. "And what do you want me to do about Millicent Burroughs? She's been calling non-stop since you pushed her meeting back."

"I'll get back to you on that one," I say. *When I remember who the hell she is*, I don't add.

"Okay, well if that's it then, I'll go and make a start," Sierra says.

"Wait," Rick says.

I hadn't noticed him sidling back over.

"Seriously, Chance? You've dragged the poor woman all the way out here and you're not even letting her take a night to herself to see the sights?" he asks.

"And that's your business because?" I ask.

He shrugs and wanders back away again.

He makes it sound like slave labor. I mean it's not like I've dragged Sierra out here against her will and her bonus will more than make up for any inconvenience. But he does have a point though. I mean it is Vegas. I smile at Sierra. "He's right," I say. "Take the night off and take in the sights. There's plenty of time tomorrow for work."

"Thank you Mr. Hunter," she says with a smile.

I return her smile and go to find the others in the bar.

SIERRA

As I head up to my room, I find that I can't get Chance out of my head. He looked so different in his jeans and t-shirt. Trendy. It's funny because he's two years younger than me, but I always think of him as older. Out of the three Hunter brothers, if I didn't know them, I would say Chance was the oldest. There's a maturity about him and he's always so well presented. But tonight he looked... different.

Don't get me wrong. I've always thought he was good looking. He has a strong jaw, full lips and beautiful blue eyes. His fair hair is always just the right amount of mussed up and he's tall and muscular. But I've never looked at him and felt myself respond to his looks like I did tonight.

Not that it matters. I mean nothing can ever happen between us. Chance is my boss and I'm not someone who acts unprofessional. Plus, he's a total workaholic and I could never be with someone who didn't have time for our relationship.

Our relationship. God, listen to me. You'd think he'd asked me out or something. All he did was give me a night off, and it's a night I would normally have had off anyway. I shake my head, pushing away my silly daydreams as I step out of the elevator and go to find my room.

I find it easily and step inside. It's nice, better than nice, luxurious. I knew it would be though. Chance had never been one to stay somewhere nice and put me somewhere cheap when we've been to conferences and stuff.

I unpack my things and take my suit off. I look at the clothes I've brought, wondering what to wear now I've got the night off. I settle on a knee length black dress and heels. I get dressed and look at myself in the mirror.

I sit down on the end of the bed. I really do want to go out and explore Vegas, but where would I go on my own? I'm kind of hungry, but sitting alone in a restaurant in Vegas is just too pathetic for words.

I decide to go for a walk along the strip and go to one of the casinos. Loads of people go to those alone, so I won't look out of place. And then I'll grab some takeout food to bring back up to my room once I'm done.

I'm humming to myself as I grab my bag and head for the door. I place my hand on the handle and a loud knock sounds from the other side. I make a startled yelping sound and then I tell myself not to be paranoid.

I open the door and my heart sinks when I see Chance standing there. I guess a night off was too much to ask for after all. It looks like it's going to be a slice of pizza while I work tonight.

CHANCE

I wake up slowly and the first thing, no, the only thing, I notice is the absolute fucking blinding pain in my head. The light streaming in the window is dazzling me and I close my eyes, trying to drift off to sleep again, but it's no use. There's no way I will be able to get to sleep with my head pounding like this. I sit up slowly, the room spinning around me. I kick my feet over the side of the bed and groan quietly.

What the fuck happened last night? Clearly, I drank far too much, but right now, it feels more like I was run over about fifty times. I blink a few times and the spinning stops. I run my hands over my face and groan again, louder this time.

A gasp from behind me startles me to my feet.

Sierra sits up, pulling the sheet up to cover her naked breasts. *Her naked breasts. What the fuck?* Even through the pain in my head and my utter confusion I can't help but notice her eyes. Without her glasses hiding them, they sparkle brightly. Even with the mascara smudges beneath them and the creases in her face from the pillow, I notice how beautiful she is. Her hair hangs around her face and over her shoulders. It's so much longer than I imagined it. It's got a slight curl to it that suits her.

"Mr. Hunter," she says, not looking at me. "What's going on?"

I think we're well past her calling me Mr. Hunter, but I don't say that. Instead, I just gape at her like an idiot for a few moments.

Her eyes flit to my face and then she looks away again.

"I-I don't know," I admit. I clear my throat awkwardly. *What the hell happened between us? Why is Sierra in my bed? And why is someone inside of my head banging away with a huge hammer?*

"Why do you keep looking at me like that?" Sierra asks quietly.

Because you're absolutely stunning and I've never noticed it before and I can't understand how I've never seen it. "I guess I'm just not used to seeing you with your hair down," I say.

I mean it literally. I've never seen Sierra without a French pleat or a tight bun in her hair.

She raises an eyebrow and looks at me, keeping her eyes firmly on my face. She gives me a half smile. "I could say the same about you," she says.

I frown, confused, and her eyes flicker down for just a second. Long enough for me to realize I am standing there completely naked, my morning wood pointing at Sierra like an accusatory finger. "Shit, sorry." I spot my boxer shorts on the ground and I grab them and pull them on.

"I feel like I've been hit by a train," Sierra says, rubbing her temples.

"Yeah. I know that feeling," I say.

"Can I use your bathroom?" she asks.

I nod.

She pulls the sheet tighter around herself. Wrapped up in it, she heads towards the bathroom door. She goes inside and closes the door.

I am still in a state of total and utter confusion, but I know I can't still be as good as naked when she comes back out, and I start to gather up my clothes.

My clothes aren't in the neat pile I would normally leave them in. They're scattered all over. That could mean one of two things though. It could mean that Sierra and I were in the throes of passion and stripping off as we moved towards the bed. Or it could mean that I was blind drunk and was just taking my clothes off at random as I moved through the room, ready to collapse into bed.

Surely, it has to be option two. That would make the most sense. I can't work out why Sierra is here though. I decide to just stop thinking about it for a moment. It's not making anything any clearer and my head is hurting worse the more I try to make sense of anything.

I pull my jeans on with a sigh. I fasten the button and as I'm pulling the zip up, a scream comes from the bathroom. I run towards the door, calling out to make sure Sierra is okay.

SIERRA

I sit down on the closed lid of the toilet, the sheet still gathered around me. My head is fuzzy, aching and I feel kind of nauseous. I can live with that though. It's only a hangover; nothing a few aspirin won't cure. The aspirin won't bring my memory back though.

What the actual fuck did I drink last night that was so potent that I have no recollection of the night before? I mean I've woken up a little disoriented before, but never in someone else's bed without knowing how I got there. And I've always been able to piece the night together after a couple of minutes.

Think Sierra I tell myself. I can't though. It's just a blank space in my head where last night should be. I can't help but think of Chance. An image flashes through my head of him standing beside the bed, his cock on show. I can't help but smile despite myself. Chance is always so together, not someone who gets rattled. But his face when he realized his cock was not only out, but was hard and pointing in my direction. If I hadn't been so embarrassed, I probably would have laughed right there and then.

I've known Chance for two years, and I've never seen him at a loss for words. He's usually so articulate. He's not a babbler, but he always knows the right thing to say for any occasion. But apparently, this morning threw him as much as it threw me, because he just stood there, his mouth opening and closing with no sound coming out.

I know we didn't have sex. Well, no actually, I don't know that. But I mean I don't think we did. Why would we? Neither of us have ever been anything but professional before. There's been no flirting, no suggestive looks. We've barely even spoken to each other except for work related things. Hell, until last night, I hadn't even seen him in casual clothes and he'd never seen me with my hair down.

Well, that's certainly all changed.

I try again to remember last night. I remember checking in to the hotel and Chance giving me the night off. So I must have left my room and went for a drink somewhere. That much is clear by the pounding in my head. So maybe I ran into Chance and the others somewhere. I mean I wouldn't have just come to his room drunk and uninvited would I?

Oh my God, would I? Did I?

Panic fills me at the thought of a drunken me knocking on Chance's room door and slurring at him. I shake my head, pushing the image away. Even if, for whatever reason, I had done that, he hadn't exactly sent me packing had he?

"I'm never drinking again," I whisper.

I get to my feet and glance into the mirror. I gasp at the state of myself. My hair is a wavy mess and I have mascara stains underneath my eyes. My skin is a dead looking grey color. *Thanks hangover.*

I can't change whatever happened last night, but I can control what happens next, at least to an extent. I can freshen up a bit and not go out there looking like I've rolled in straight out of the trash.

I turn the cold tap on, clutching the sheet with one hand. I wet the other hand and run it over my hair, taming the worst of the wavy bits. *Oh, who am I kidding?* They're not wavy bits. They're frizzy bits. I rub at the mascara underneath my eyes. I manage to get the most of it off.

I tuck the sheet in on itself, so both of my hands are free as I cup water into my hands and splash it onto my face. I'm starting to feel a little more human now. I reach out to turn the tap off and a flash of gold catches my eye.

My eyes widen and panic fills my whole body.

"No, no, no," I whisper.

Pre-order the book here:
Tangled with the CEO

ABOUT THE AUTHOR

Thank you so much for reading!
If you have enjoyed the book and would like to leave a
precious review for me, please kindly do so here:

Untangle My Heart

Please click on the link below to receive info about my latest
releases and giveaways.
NEVER MISS A THING

Or
come and say hello here:

ALSO BY IONA ROSE

Made in the USA
Middletown, DE
18 May 2022